HIGH STRANGENESS

TALES FROM THE EDGE OF THE UNKNOWN

A CHILLING COLLECTION

BY

PHILIP TICE

COVER ILLUSTRATION BY

NUNO SARNADAS

Table of Contents

THE IN-BETWEEN

Welcome to the In-Between World

Operating from 10:17 P.M. to 1:59 A.M.,

Beginning when couches become just too comfortable
 to get up and go anywhere

And ending mere seconds before the drunken throngs conduct
their barroom exodus,

returning, like staggering phantoms, to their respective places
of rest.

But those who venture into the In-Between enter a twilight world

A stagnant limbo

Where nothing has yet happened,

But absolutely everything soon will.

Between these witching hours, the world bares its claws and rises
on its haunches,

Her pounce yet to explode from its shadowed perch.

It is a land of perpetual anticipation.

Where the breath of the world is held, chaste and still.

The weather of the In-Between mirrors the rest of this topsy
turvey domain,

The air hangs hot and heavy on passersby's' skin like the breath
of a lover

Consummation only inches away, satisfaction never to come.

The dark sky is cramping and pregnant with storm, crowning but
not yet arrived.

Some trickles of rain dribble down to the limbo below,

And all eyes turn to the clouds, watching for the true birth

Will it be born light and tearless?

Only spattering the earth with a sweet summer drizzle?

Or will a thunderous Caesarian rip open the heavens

and unleash furious gusts and sharp tongues of lightning from
its womb?

Unfortunately, that is a question for the 2 A.M. crowd.

This is the In-Between

And though you may be our guest

You are required to play by our rules,

no matter how alien they may seem.

For you see, the In-Between is a balance:

Between night and day

Between dreams and whispers

Between life and death

Put your ear to the wind, go ahead

There is no music, but there is no silence

Here the ear is greeted by a symphony of hushed promises

and the hypnotic lapping of a black river

By radio static on the rain and deadbolts making their
nocturnal retreat

Even the cars, the streetlamps, the mouthless things on these
shadowed streets

Sings to each other, here in the In-Between

Though curiously, they never seem to get any closer

or any louder than passing spirits in the night

Chanting…

"Welcome to the In-Between
We know you can't stay long
We would love for you to join us
In the chorus of our midnight song."

THE DINER AT THE EDGE
OF NOWHERE

THE HIGHWAY STRETCHED OUT in front of me for arduous miles, just as it had for the interminable hour before. These South Jersey country highways were all like this, especially late at night – dead empty, save for the odd filling stations and the scraggle trees of the Pine Barrens that line the road's forlorn shoulder. It had been a long time since I had been down a road like this, in a night as deep as this one – I would've avoided this rural stretch entirely if I could, but there was some sort of construction on the Parkway that sent me down this backwater detour. I knew my home state's roadways were notorious for their constant state of accepted disrepair, but 3 A.M. is late for that sort of work, even for Jersey's famously bemoaned highwaymen.

It had been a long time since I had returned to New Jersey – I was born here and grew up in the Northern tip of the state, closer to the sprawling metropolitan maw of New York City. These Pine Barren swamplands were about as foreign to me as the surface of the moon as far as I was concerned. The only times I ventured down this far south was when I was a boy, and my family would visit a little Ocean County amusement park called *Wizard's Village*. It was a ramshackle collection of gnome-themed kiddie roller coasters and little snack stands in the shape of toadstools, tucked away in the forests outside of Barnegat – unremarkable but with a particular home-grown charm.

We stopped visiting Wizard's Village when I was about 8 or 9, and last I had heard, the elderly owner – Mr. Mustafa – had passed away a few years back. He built most of the Village with his own two hands and had run the old spot for something like forty years before suddenly dropping dead a few summers back. His children, having no interest in the upkeep of the already-struggling wonderland, allowed Wizard's Village to decay and be devoured by the Pinelands at its gates. I thought about swinging by, to pay my respects to Mustafa's abandoned dream for old times' sake – but the magic was long gone, and there was no way I was going to wander around the creepy husk of that old amusement park when the sun was already so low in the sky. I let the Village's remote highway exit pass me by and continued my way through the crisp New Jersey twilight.

I was born in the Garden State, but I've spent most of my adult life in California or out on the open road as a writer, searching this great wide world for a publisher with the slightest interest in my work. I write fiction mostly – beatnik stories about the increasingly elusive everyperson, like the ones that once captivated the imaginations of readers back in Steinbeck's day. Stories about wanderers like me. Unfortunately, there's not much of a market for rambling accounts of directionless wayfarers anymore, so I make ends meet writing pulpy true crime stories or paperback biographies of baseball players I've never heard of before – you can pick them up wherever your cheapest drug store dime novels are sold. But I don't want those to be my legacy, even if they are my meal tickets.

Tonight, I attended a publisher's conference down in Atlantic City, in some dried-up old casino named The Pink Pearl. It was a leftover relic from the coastal city's gambling heyday, gutted to make room for drab gray conference halls and nickel slot machines to entertain the passing hordes of pensioners that descended upon the casino weekly with their retirement home chauffeurs. The plan was to rub elbows and brown noses at this publisher's conference in hopes of getting my latest manuscript off the ground.

I won't bore you with the details, but this new book was the first thing I'd written in a long while that I felt has some substance, maybe even something important to say — so naturally, it was rejected outright by every pig headed, splotch-cheeked publisher in the place. Even after a night of buying them house liquor and heat lamp appetizers out of my own pocket, I couldn't get a single one to even read the damned thing. To add insult to injury, they weren't even New York publishers — the bastards were from Philadelphia.

Now I was driving down this dark state road, on my way back North to crash on an old friend's couch and grab whatever scraps of shut eye I could before I had to catch a train up to Boston to try this shtick all over again at some publisher's convention in the Foxwoods. Before I left the Pearl I called my agent, Jerry, from one of the casino's pay phones to inform him of my crushing defeat. Jerry had few kind words to say before my coinage ran dry, but he scolded me yet again for trying to traffic my new manuscript as my 'one-and-only' story to tell. He told me — nay, commanded me — to write another book or two so I could walk into my next pitch with a repertoire of work and avoid looking like a one-trick-pony at the next meeting of the minds. To appease him, I surrendered to Jerry and told him that I would have another story for him by the time I made it back to Los Angeles, after the East Coast had thoroughly chewed me up and spit me out. The prodigal son's return to the Garden State was not going as planned.

But at this time of night, I couldn't think about new books, or Jerry, or Foxwoods — hell, I could barely keep my eyes from drifting back and forth across the highway center line, and I feared my steering wheel would soon follow suit if I didn't find a way to wake myself. It didn't help that The Pearl's vodka cranberries had left me with a mind-numbing headache that made my brain feel like a mason jar that someone had taken it upon themselves to fill with wasps and give a good hard shaking.

As my car trudged on through the forested night, the fill stations along the side of the road began to trickle away into nothingness; the few cars that had once shared the lonely road with me all disappeared into the blackness; even the streetlamps seemed further and further apart as I delved deeper into the Barrens, leaving me alone with just my headlights and the glinting eyes of lurking forest creatures to lead me through the silent expanse. Soon enough, my head grew heavy and my eyes grew dim and I knew I was at the doorstep of an ultimatum – I either needed to find myself some gas station coffee in the next few miles, or I had to pull over to the shoulder to sleep off my stupor until the morning light, which would put me dangerously close to missing my New England-bound train. But anything was better than running my car off the road and sinking in some forgotten marsh pit.

The Pinelands were a well-known place of death – its thick muck and labyrinthine undergrowth made the marshes a perfect No Man's Land for lost hikers and mobster hit-jobs to meet their fates, their missing bodies never to be found amongst the smothering grip of those endless, twisting trees. Those lost causes, those sacrifices to Barrens – I was determined to avoid joining their faceless ranks tonight.

Just as a highway shoulder slumber began to look more and more appealing, my tired eyes were greeted by a buzzing, holy glow, shimmering through the damp glass of my windshield – up ahead on the side of the road was a diner!

It was a classic, chrome-plated 50's diner, one of the countless that Jersey was so famous for, though this particular eatery seemed to have little to champion as 'famous'. It was a stout structure surrounded by a gravel parking lot, above which loomed a neon sign that read *The Railyard Diner* in crackling red font, next to a rusted train track crossing light to hammer the diner's theme home. Perhaps a deposed train depot sat hidden amongst the trees somewhere around here – this diner might have once serviced its workers before the railway shut down or the big highway was built and left this little town to wallow in obscurity like many ill-fated settlements that dotted these woods.

I didn't mind one bit, though – I was but a castaway and this misfit was the salvation I had been searching for. Just in the nick of time. It was a gift from The Jersey Devil to make up for my terrible luck up until this point, because any true native knows that there is no substance more potent than a cup of Jersey diner coffee to bring your soul back from the brink.

I rolled my car into the gravel lot next to a few other beat-up pickup trucks and wood paneled sedans – dated relics like the establishment itself. Strangely enough, it seemed I wasn't the only night owl to have stumbled across this nocturnal outpost hidden deep in the Pines. I brought my pad and pen with me, hoping some inspiration might strike between cups of joe – who knows, maybe one of these graveyard shift stragglers had a tale to tell.

The gravel crunched under my heels as I made the brisk walk from my car to the diner's front door, next to which dangled a creased "*Yes We're Open!*" sign, faded from perpetual use. Upon stepping out of my car, I felt the cold September air bite my face and the wind bombard my senses with the smells of pine needles and wood-rot. Animals chirped and chattered just out of sight, moving deftly amongst the encroaching shadows, the hoots of owls and the cackling of jackals seeming to mock me from afar. The wings of some nocturnal thing flapped above me but disappeared amongst the pine boughs quicker than I could spot it. I could feel the eyes of the night on me, hear the whispers of the Barrens creeping into my ears and up the back of my skull… this witching hour was far more alive than I had anticipated, but my unseen observers remained hidden beyond the diner's neon halo. I was unnerved, and though my journey was only a matter of a few strides, I crossed the lot as quickly as I could, longing for the safety inside.

Cha-ring! A tiny tin bell danced above the door as I entered the Rail-yard Diner. The diner's interior was exactly what I expected – identical to what you find in every diner up and down the Garden State, as if there was only one true Jersey diner, echoed over and over again along every stretch of highway across the state.

It was a modest restaurant, split into two sections – the first was a café area, where one found a couple tables and chairs scattered across the checkerboard tile floor. At the rear of the room sat the diner's counter, lined with day-old muffins under glass domes, scorched coffee pots, and bottles of obscure Greek liquors, all presided over by a gruff, towering chef with thick black eyebrows and an oil-stained t-shirt. Through a metal slit behind the bar, you could peer into the kitchen, but most of the kitchen lights were off, giving only glimpses of glinting steel in the shadows beyond.

The other portion of the diner was the dining room, a green-carpeted space partially obscured by a wall of frosted glass panes, behind which sat a number of red-leather booths. Empty from the looks of it. Next to the dining room door, a rainbow-lined jukebox sat silent, a 45" record raised on its thin metal arm, waiting for a quarter's permission to play a tune... any tune...

There were only a few patrons in the diner, corresponding to the number of cars out in the lot. As I took in the little restaurant, I clocked each straggler – there was the chef behind the counter, a brutish truck driver at the end of the bar mulling over a bowl of chili, and an elderly man in a bare tweed jacket sharing a booth with a small mutt as mangy as he was. Across from his booth sat a swooning teenage couple, the bright-eyed young girl wrapped in her boyfriend's varsity football jacket, their faces never more than a few inches apart. Some other silhouetted shapes moved formlessly behind the dining room's frosted glass panes, but I couldn't make out much detail. They were all typical fare for a place like this – outcasts, runaways, and night owls. Diners have always been safe havens for the people on the fringes.

Before I could take more than a few steps through the door and onto the scuffed linoleum floor, I was intercepted by a little old woman with a wide smile that caused her wrinkles to crumple in on themselves, nearly absorbing the rest of her kindly face into her grinning folds. She was dressed in a black-and-white shirtwaist dress, affixed with the traditional white triangle collars and sauce-peppered apron – she seemed as if she had stepped right out of 1955, her pointed horn-rimmed glasses completing the look. Right beneath her collar, she had the name "Nora" sewn on her lapel in a dainty cursive font, though its loose ends and fraying strands suggested the getup had seen better days.

"Well, hello there, stranger," Nora beamed. As she walked over to me, I saw that she was wiping some sticky, black substance off of her hands with a ratty white rag she kept holstered in her apron. Probably fryer grease or something. "Welcome to the Railyard Diner – what brings you in today?"

"Just passing through and thought I'd come in for a pick-me-up. How's your night, Nora?" I smiled, peppering her name into the conversation – people feel special when you do little things like that. I've always taken pride in being able to choose my words for maximum effect, to endear myself to new people. Now if only that charm worked on my publishers…

"My night is just fine, thanks for asking," Nora smiled even wider – she radiated a strong maternal energy, as if she was the doting grandmother of all the patrons that passed through her doors. "I think we can get you set with that pick me up. Any preference on where you'd like to sit, Scott?"

"The counter would be just fine—" I answered, almost without thinking. But it wasn't until Nora grabbed a laminated menu and began to walk towards the counter that I stopped dead in my tracks on one of the black checker floor tiles. "Wait, how did you know my name?"

I hadn't introduced myself, and I didn't have my name stitched into my lapel like my elderly hostess. But Nora just turned her head and gave a knowing wink before continuing towards the barstools, answering over her shoulder: "Your notebook, son,"

I looked down. I had taken my notepad into the diner with me, and the little cardboard cover did have my name scrawled in blue pen ink on its face – but the writing was small and crooked, thanks to my abysmal penmanship. How the old waitress had been able to read it from behind the hostess stand was beyond me... but maybe those horn-rimmed glasses were more powerful than I had thought.

Nora placed me at one of the red-leather barstools at the center of the back counter, laying a menu down next to me. The stool creaked and crunched under my weight, the old thing sitting somewhat lopsided on its pole.

"Now, you just take a look at what you'd like and Rufus here will get you all settled," Nora instructed, leaving me with the chef as she returned to her post.

I glanced at the cover of the menu, but quickly disregarded it – any New Jersey native worth their salt doesn't need a menu at a roadside diner. You order by intuition alone! It also helps that every diner in Jersey serves pretty much the exact same things, as if they were all a part of a grand conspiracy to spread disco fries to every corner of the great Garden State. No, I would only need the basics tonight.

"Just a coffee, please. Black," I said to Rufus, the towering chef. Up close, I could see that Rufus was more Sasquatch than man, his arms overgrown with matted tufts of black hair leading up to his monolithic head, where one would find an unkempt black beard that clawed its way up his oblong cheeks to the crown of his skull, atop which sat a faded blue hairnet. His eyes were piercing, set so deep in his head that his sockets seemed to make their own cavernous shadows. "And a slice of cherry pie, too, if you have any."

Rufus made no noise, issued no acknowledgement of my order, but I saw in his gaze that he had heard me. Wordlessly, he scribbled down my order on a waiter's pad, tore the sheet free, and hooked it onto a little turnstile atop the kitchen window behind him. As he poured my cup of coffee from a dented tin kettle, I heard a metallic creak, and when I next looked up to the turnstile, the order slip was gone, assumedly snatched by the kitchen worker dwelling somewhere in the darkness on the other side of the wall.

Before I could think much about it, Rufus set my cup of coffee down in front of me, the clacking of the saucer on the counter bringing my attention back to the beverage at hand. Despite my thanks, Rufus still remained silent, his contemptible gaze seeming to say: "*Just because I'm behind this counter doesn't mean I have to like you.*" And I couldn't blame him – the graveyard shift must be brutal, especially on a forgotten stretch of road such as this one.

As the coffee's aroma floated up from beneath my nose to greet me, my exhausted body suddenly wired by the very hint of caffeine – but I restrained myself from gulping down the piping hot liquid that very second, no matter how much I may have wanted to. I could wait another minute for it to cool – I didn't need a dead tongue on top of all of my other troubles.

"… *Hspshazsksph…*" I heard faint whispers murmur in my left ear, their words barely audible, much less decipherable. I turned my head towards the sound, unsure if I had actually heard anything at all – it had felt like the sensation you feel when you think you hear your name called in the midst of a crowd. But the only other living soul to my left was the aforementioned truck driver, clad in a red plaid overshirt, still hovering over his untouched chili – surely he hadn't said anything to me. Hell, I wasn't sure if the man was even awake – his eyes were difficult to make out from beneath the brim of his worn ballcap – but for an overnight trucker like him, I imagined you had to grab whatever morsels of sleep you could, when you could.

Rather than disturb the poor man and still waiting on my coffee to cool, I turned my head in the other direction, just in time to see the teen-age couple giggle to each other before disappearing into the dining room, possibly off to find a more private spot where their necking could continue unobserved. I remembered doing the same thing when I was their age, sneaking off with a girl to steal kisses behind the waiter's partition at the Scotchwood Diner…

Better times. Or, at least, simpler ones.

However, my reminiscing was soon interrupted by a sound from the old tweed man's booth – it was the whining of his mutt. The scrappy little thing was bounding back on its hind legs, whimpering for a scrap of food from its master. The old man cooed, shushing the animal before returning his eyes to a folded photograph he rubbed gingerly between his fingers. The photo was small, wallet sized, black and white – or at least so faded that it appeared to be. I couldn't make out the subject in the weathered picture, but I thought I saw a lonely tear roll down the old man's sunken leather cheek. However, with a quick wipe from his palm, the evidence of the teardrop was gone.

I felt the metal curls of my notebook binding and I considered walking over to the old timer and asking for his story – after all, I had told Jerry I would get him something usable – but before I could rise off my stool, a voice stopped me cold:

"What're you doing here, boy?"

I turned over my shoulder, following the growling voice to the far end of the bar. There my eyes found a ragged man, dressed in a shredded coat and an ill-fitting, sweat-putrefied shirt draped over his sharp bones. Ratty stubble jutted from his chattering chin and a head of matted, oily hair fell over his face, almost obscuring his rabid, bloodshot eyes. He looked like a junkie or some marsh person, trailing his own muck along with him from the depths of the Barrens. Maybe he was some poor local – someone the kids in North Jersey would've called a 'Piney'.

I was stunned momentarily – I hadn't seen the Piney when I had walked in. Maybe he had been hiding out in the bathroom, shooting up in the corner of some stall for the last twenty minutes or murmuring to himself in the mirror. I glanced around to see if there was anyone else the Piney could've possibly been talking to, but the other patrons hadn't even turned their heads to acknowledge the wildman's existence – maybe this was an example of that famous Jersey 'not-my-problem' attitude, but something wasn't right. When my gaze cautiously returned to the Piney, his pupils quickly snapped to meet me. I was his prey now.

"You heard me," he hissed, as if whispering some great secret. "Why are you here?"

"I was just passing through –," I replied tenuously, but my words were barely past my lips before the Piney leapt back into the conversation.

"Well you'd better keep on passing! While you still can," he glared, his hair shifting like a den of snakes as he shot paranoid glances around the rest of the diner. Still nothing from the other patrons. "Before *they* don't let you…"

"*They* who?" I leaned in, placing my notebook back on the counter, wondering how difficult it would be to write notes without the crazed man noticing. This Piney was on some sort of ride in his own mind, but maybe I could bottle some of that insanity and make it into something I could use. "Are *they* here?"

"They're everywhere. They're in every room. They're in the cups. They're on the road. They're back there," the Piney explained, his eyes never breaking their dead stare aimed at the shadowed kitchen window, as if something was lurking back there and his gaze was all that was keeping it at bay. "But do you know what's scaring me most?"

"What is it?" I pushed, keeping my expression nebulous – but inside, I was dying to know the cryptic man's secret.

"I… I think…," the Piney murmured, turning his eyes back to me. For the first time, they softened, the grip of fear rendering him – well – human. Warm tears welled in his panicked eyes as he gathered his thoughts into speech:

"I think they've burrowed in my stomach. I think they're inside me."

I scribbled down a note with my free hand, keeping my eyes locked on the Piney – I could decipher my blind scrawlings later. This man's story was too bizarre to pass up.

"That pretty wild, man," was all I could think to say. "When did you start to think they were after you?" I followed up, trying to stoke the Piney into an even more energized tale. Absentmindedly, I took a sip of my coffee – my tongue recoiled upon contact, the drink coating my tongue with a sour, almost ashen flavor. But before I could process the strange aftertaste, the Piney whipped toward me, fury gripping every muscle in his scarecrow body.

"NO!" he hollered and leapt from his stool, tackling me to the ground and smashing the coffee mug, the drink splashing across the monotone floor tiles. The Piney gnashed his teeth, tearing at me, descending into a pure frenzy. He foamed at the mouth and howled unintelligible words as he fluctuated between cries and moans.

"They burrow! They burrow! In your marrow! In your brain!" the Piney wailed. "In the Forever Wood they dwell! Feeding, changing! You can't let them in!"

The Piney cried out, raising his fists high over his head and prepared to deliver a blow directly to my skull – I had been in a fight or two before, but crazed strength is something you should never underestimate. Seeing an opening, I cracked the madman across his jaw with a clumsy punch, freeing myself from beneath his legs and sending two of his teeth clattering across the floor. As I pulled myself to my feet, Rufus restrained the Piney, the other patrons finally acknowledging the scuffle.

But I didn't care if I had backup – I was gone! One of the Piney's gold capped teeth glinted on the checkerboard floor, as if issuing a sinister wink to bid me goodbye as I stumbled out the diner door.

I thought I heard Nora calling out something behind me, but I wasn't waiting around to hear her. The Piney's attack had shocked my system into action, so I was in my car, key turned, and peeling out of the gravel lot before my brain had time to keep up. In the chaos, I wasn't even sure which direction I was driving down the highway – I just needed to get out of there as fast as my wheels could carry me!

After a few minutes of white-knuckling the steering wheel, my grip loosened and my breathing began to slow, the adrenaline beginning to work its way out of my blood. I began to take in my surroundings again, clocking the dark road ahead of me, now completely devoid of light, save for my meager headlights. As the shadows fed into one another, morphing enigmatically in the underbrush at the corners of my vision, I realized that I was barreling even deeper into the Barrens. The forest swallowed even the moon, and soon my only companions were the long shadows of corrupted pine trees that threatened to engulf the county road.

"No problem," I assured myself, "Soon I'll hit a crossroad, find my bearings, and be back on the interstate in no time. This isn't that long of a road."

But the crossroads didn't appear. I drove and I drove, but I found no cross streets, no fill stations, no houses – nothing. Nothing but the endless Pine Barrens. Until finally, I saw a glow in the distance, near the side of the road.

"Thank God..." I whispered aloud. My paranoia had started to take hold inside the cramped little car cabin, but this sight assuaged my fears ... until I drove closer and saw the source of the light:

It was The Railyard Diner, still standing as a neon outpost on the edge of the nothingness. Somehow, the winding forest road had led me right back to where I had started. Locals have always claimed that the Pines have a way of getting people turned around, especially outsiders, especially at night. But ... I had just driven straight ahead! I didn't even remember taking a turn. How did I end up back here?

Spotting a side road jutting off into the woods just past the diner, I made the split-second decision to take it! Slamming my foot on the gas, I turned hard and began to rumble down the forest path, with no regard for how my little suburban car would handle the unkempt rural road. The pavement was shattered and poxed with holes as low-hanging pine branches whipped and cracked their dry fingers against my windshield, my mad escape surely leaving a trail of severed tree limbs in my wake. But I didn't care, and I had no intention of looking back. My gaze was locked ahead as my speedometer needle climbed ever higher, my eyes constantly scanning for danger – if an unexpected deer was to step out from the undergrowth, my only choice would be to go through the poor thing. But I was starting to believe the claims that stranger things than deer lurked in the Pines.

Just as the brush threatened to swallow me whole, I saw my light reflect off something in the darkness – something metal. Choking my emergency brake and spitting rubble into the night, I wrestled my car to a stop, my engine wheezing with a panic that mirrored my own. But as I looked out my window, I felt a bright spark of hope leap in my chest – the metal glint was coming from a police car, sitting idle amongst the creaking trees!

As I clambered out of my vehicle with a healthy dose of glances thrown over my shoulder, I realized that the police cruiser was an older model, with a boxy snout and a bar of cherrytop lights atop its hood. It looked closer to something out of the 1970s, but that wasn't uncommon for the Pine Barrens – in these parts, you made do with whatever hand-me-downs and fixer-uppers you could find.

As I inched closer, I could make out a single silhouette in the driver's seat and a crackle of a police scanner floating on the night breeze – there was someone inside!

"Officer! Officer!" I cried out, my overwhelming relief trumping my self-preservation instincts as I ran towards the cruiser. "Hey, there's something weird going on around here – can you tell me how to get back to the highway? I'm all turned around and…"

My voice trailed away like smoke on the cold autumn wind as I reached the driver's side door and realized the cop hadn't even acknowledged me – instead, he stared straight ahead, mumbling into the radio transceiver gripped tight between his frigid pale fingers.

"Officer Allen calling all available units…" the cop spoke, his voice slurring like a man half asleep. "Requesting back up on Old Mill Road…"

No voice pierced the hissing radio static with a reply. Just as I was about to reach out to grab the officer's attention, he began to repeat himself – with the exact same rhythm and the exact same cadence, as if he was some malfunctioning record skipping on an errant scratch. But this time I noticed something I hadn't gleaned upon my first listen – there was an undercurrent of quivering dread beneath his words, as if he might break into tears at any provocation.

"Officer Allen calling all available units… Requesting backup on Old Mill Road…"

Again, the officer's pleas for reinforcements were met with unflinching silence. Just as I sensed he was about to repeat himself for a third time, I grabbed the cop's arm through his open window, interrupting his loop.

"Officer," I spoke forcefully, hoping my words would pierce whatever stupor had him in his grip. "Where's the highway? What the hell are you doing here?"

My words seemed to burrow through the officer's haze as I clocked a shift in the man's face, his shadowed, stoic expression shifting into a look of befuddlement as he processed my question… as if he had never expected to hear another human's voice again.

"The road is… up the…," the officer stammered, taking in his surroundings for the first time with the bafflement of a man emerging from a coma for the first time in years. "I don't remember… everything's foggy…"

As the officer turned his head, terror seized me and I released my grip on the cop's arm, tumbling backwards onto the dusty forest floor as my headlights illuminated the man's features. His face was ashen, with unnatural blue lips and violet veins creeping across his translucent skin, like a frostbitten corpse left to the mercy of the elements. But it was his eyes, frosted over with a milky white glaze, staring forward with their unseeing pupils that put the fear of God in my heart and propelled me back into my driver's seat.

As I threw my car into gear and spun gravel beneath my wheels, I heard Officer Allen moan one last thing before my engine carried me deeper into the woods and out of sight:

"Please... I don't know where I am..."

I sped away, ashamed that I had left the tormented officer stranded in the depths of the Barrens — but on a night like tonight, my only focus was getting myself out of this crooked place alive. As far as I was concerned, all the other poor bastards stuck here were already too far gone.

Thankfully, the reflective eyes of the night wildlife kept far away from my growling motor until I finally spotted a T-junction in a clearing ahead, the forest path connecting back to a main road. My headlights burst from the brush as my rear tires buckled and skidded to a halt in the middle of the street, exploding out of the pines with the energy of a frightened child running up the stairs after turning off his basement lights.

My car thrummed beneath me as I caught my breath in a series of heavy, labored gasps. As the adrenaline-tainted confusion in my brain began to clear, I focused on my hands and realized they were bathed in a deep red glow. I looked down at my lap, my chest — all of me shimmered with otherworldly crimson light. Panning my eyes up through my branch-scratched windshield, my heart plummeted into a pit deeper than I thought my chest could contain and a scream clawed its way to the very peak of my throat. I don't know if that scream escaped my mouth or if it just reverberated through my brain, but in that moment, fear was all I knew.

There in front of me, casting the ethereal, bloodstained glow, was a twisting neon script that read: R A I L Y A R D. I had found myself at the foot of the diner yet again, or perhaps it was the diner that had found me.

Defeated, I just sat in the road, my engine grumbling beneath me, waiting for instructions I couldn't bear to give. I didn't care if a truck came along and made me into an ugly little smear on the pavement – at least then I wouldn't have to worry about figuring a way out of whatever horrible backroad limbo I had found myself in.

Convinced that there must be a way back to true civilization, perhaps known only to the entrenched locals, I saw no other choice but to pull back into the gravel lot and ask for directions from the diner patrons, hopeful that my attacker had since fled off into the forest to rejoin the other beasts of the night.

Cha-ring! The tin bell over the door rang the same as it had before, but this time I felt no welcome in its chime. The restaurant seemed relatively undisturbed, the diners inside making no noise, save for the occasional yipping from the old man's pup. There was no sign of the Piney or our earlier brawl – the tiled floor remained unscathed.

"Ah, Scott!" Nora beamed, trotting out from the back of the diner through the swinging kitchen doors. I tried to sneak a glance into the shrouded kitchen beyond, but the shadows remained impenetrable.

"You left us in such a hurry, you didn't pay for your coffee," she fussed, her plastered smile never leaving her face, "And you didn't even get your pie!"

"Oh well, that... that man at the counter –," I started to explain, stammering to collect my scattered thoughts. But my words dried up when I turned my head back towards the diner counter and saw a steaming, ruby red piece of cherry pie, sitting on a pristine white saucer, right in front of the stool where I had been sitting. I swore that the pie hadn't there when I walked in just seconds ago.

"Oh, that rude fella – I'm sorry you had to deal with that, son. This deep out in the Pines… well, all sorts of people can come out of those woods, you know," Nora assured me, a trickle of poison seeping into her grin at the mention of the delinquent Piney. Without waiting for my reply, Nora guided me back to my stool at the counter, Rufus' dark gaze never waning, never blinking. But nevertheless, I followed – I still needed those directions if I wanted to escape the Pine Barrens before sunrise.

"I was actually wondering if you could point me in the direction of the highway," I tried to explain as I cautiously lowered myself back onto the creaking barstool. "You see I –"

"Got turned around, did ya?" Nora scoffed, surely amused by this outsider's ignorance. "Happens to you city folk pretty often. But don't worry, I think I've got a highway map over at the hostess stand. I'll mark you up some directions and getcha on your way."

"In the meantime, you just enjoy that pie," Nora winked before strolling back over to the hostess stand. I breathed a shallow sigh of relief – despite the humiliation of trudging back to the diner after my less-than-heroic exit, it seemed I would finally be out of this godforsaken place soon. Maybe the sugar from the pie would be enough to hold me over until I could get to a Motel 6 or something. Anywhere but here.

Resigned to my fate, I spooned a corner of the pie into my mouth, letting the sugary preserves melt over my tongue. The crust was flaky, the fruit sweet … but there was a tinny aftertaste, like the pie innards had begun to rust. I flinched at the metallic flavor, but maybe my fork was to blame. I looked around for my coffee cup to wash the pastry down, but I soon remembered it had been smashed in the fight with the Piney. Rufus seemed to clock my confusion and spoke his first words of the entire night:

"New cup," the behemoth man grunted, grabbing a fresh mug from the dishwashing station. I nodded in appreciation and returned for a second mouthful of pie. As I chewed, I watched Rufus place the mug in front of me and begin to refill the cup with his nearby kettle – but as the coffee poured forth, it spilled out of the kettle mouth in viscous chunks, like curdled milk left to rot, slopping down into the mug where the dark ichor burbled like an oily tar pit.

Before my brain could process the unnatural sight and relay the message to my jaw muscles, I chewed the mouthful of pie one last time – and was greeted by a chilling crunch inside my own skull. Reaching into my gums, I latched onto something jagged, something solid. Something that had been inside the pie until a moment before…

When I removed my fingers, they were dripping with crimson pulp, clutching a human tooth, topped with a golden crown filling – but the tooth wasn't mine. It was the same tooth I had punched free from the Piney's mouth during our fight!

My eyes dropped to the counter to find the sinister dessert staring back at me – literally. Inside the pastry's gory filling was the yellowed, beady eye of the Piney, glaring back in my direction, the pupil darting around the room with demented energy, still alive!

"GAHH!" I gasped, fright electrifying my body as I tried in vain to swallow my cry, the shock sending me toppling off my barstool and splaying out across the checkered floor. My flailing arms brought the coffee mug smashing down beside me, but the moment the black liquid was freed from its container, the tar frantically crawled its way across the floor and slithered under the kitchen door, propelled by its own alien will.

Suddenly, the few noises that had still echoed through the diner hushed to an eerie silence. Utensils ceased their clinking and, as my eyes darted around the café room, I was met with the most bloodcurdling sights – it seemed that now that I was aware of whatever nightmares lived in this place, a veil had been lifted, and unthinkable horrors laid beyond.

"… *Hspshazsksph*…" I again heard the slithering whispers on the wind, and this time, my hyper-alert senses were able to follow the sound… back to the truck driver at the end of the counter. The whispers continued, hissing and gurgling with increasing voracity, but not once did the trucker's mouth move to say them. But he did obey them.

Without any change in expression, the trucker carefully unbuttoned his plaid shirt, revealing his bare chest beneath – the source of the muffled whispers, growing more ravenous with each undone button. As the shirt fell open, the whispers could wait no longer – the trucker's chest tore open, his skin flaying and tearing horizontally from his naval to his collarbone as a faceless, many-fanged mouth ripped forth from his body! Pairs of tendrils burst from his sides and shoveled the bowl of chili into the fleshy maw, the creature devouring cutlery and all, pulsing like an engorged mealworm. During all this, the trucker's face never changed, and then I realized he was not even a man – just a flesh vehicle for the monster within.

I wanted to run, to stand and flee back out into the endless night, but my legs had lost their strength and my synapses were too petrified to fire. I crawled across the tiles away from the horrors at the counter, but soon found myself at the foot of the old tweed man's table, his jittery mutt chattering in front of my nose. It whined and begged, the chaos only seeming to further provoke the dog's hunger. The old man sighed, finally succumbing to his pet's prodding:

"Alright, alright," he conceded, the old man's voice groaning its way from his withered lips with the coarseness of gravel under car tires. With a resigned nod, the old man folded the age-bleached photograph back into his coat pocket, before reaching down and wrapping his skeletal fingers around his boney wrist – before ripping off his arm free from his body! The shriveled limb tore away with the ease of ripping a straw appendage off of a forgotten scarecrow, and the old man dropped it down to the dog. The animal yipped with delight and quickly began to gnaw at the exposed radius bone mere inches away from my face.

The sight was enough to propel me back to my feet, my adrenaline firing me towards the diner door – but out of the corner of my eye, I could see the tweed man's face relax into a relieved smile, despite the dangling sinew still hanging from his shoulder as not blood, but sand, poured from his wound.

I reached the glass door, slamming against the handle with all the momentum my body could deliver, but the flimsy door refused to budge. The tin bell refused to ring. Try as I might, I could not pry the door open, and even after delivering a flurry of frantic fists and elbows, the glass remained undisturbed. But my frenzy had drawn the attention of Rufus and his dark eyes. Fearful of what the giant might do if he were to catch me, I turned on my heels and ducked past the frosted glass into the dining room, but I soon realized I was no better off there either.

When I had looked past that murky glass earlier in the night, all I had seen were the incoherent shadows of patrons on the other side – and that was exactly what I found waiting for me as I stumbled into the arena of scarlet leather booths. In front of me, a dozen silhouettes sat at the various tables, their forms vaguely suggesting that they had once been something human, but their bodies became distorted and jagged when they moved, as if the shadows were being played back on a damaged VHS tape. They crackled and moaned upon seeing me, their faceless groanings echoing as if wailed from the depths of some deep, dark cave.

In the corner of the dining room, I spotted the teenage couple, the pop of color from their varsity jacket drawing my attention away from the static men. The couple were in the throes of passion in their booth, kissing with such ferocity that they completely ignored the dark forces just feet away from their date night. But just as I considered running to the kids, tearing them apart and telling them to run – *run before it's too late!* – the girl sensed my entrance and finally broke the lip lock, revealing a sight that chilled me where I stood.

When she turned to face me, her features were warped and distorted: two sets of pupils floated in the whites of her eyes, two noses drifted aimlessly around her face as two sets of lopsided lips linked together rows of lopsided teeth, her whole head morphing and dripping like candlewax.

The boyfriend also turned to look at me, but his face was completely gone – with no features and no mouth, the boy's face looked like a blank drum skin pulled taught over a smooth skull. Though he had no eyes, I could feel his stare cut straight through me. Smelling my fear, the girl grinned a hideous, lopsided grin and began to giggle. It was the same giggle I had heard from both of them when I had first arrived – but this time, both voices came laughing out of the same mouth. Her mouth.

Worried that I would be driven fully, irrevocably insane if I was to look upon the girl's nightmarish Picasso face another second longer, I swallowed my terror and hobbled to the only possible haven left – the bathroom at the back of the dining room!

I barreled through the black bathroom door, quickly slamming it shut behind me. The knob locked from the inside, thank God, and I even dragged the bathroom's heavy metal trash can over in front of the entrance just to make doubly sure nothing could break through – or, at least, that's what I hoped. For the first time in minutes, I had a moment to collect myself and catch my breath.

The bathroom was small, equipped with a singular porcelain toilet in the corner and a rust-peppered sink in front of the door, overlooked by a weathered old mirror adorned with small graffiti scratchings. I flicked the nearby light switch, but the single pitiful bulb that hung above my head had long since burnt out its last filament. However, the darkness revealed a shaft of pale moonlight, shining through the small window at the top of the bathroom wall!

I ran to it, using whatever strength I could muster to scramble up the slick tiled wall and reach the windowsill, hoping that it would prove to be my final salvation! But as I flung the window open, I was devastated to find that it was so narrow that only my arm would fit through the slit. I pushed and contorted my body, tears welling in my eyes, my shoulder feeling as though it would nearly pop out of its socket – but it was no use.

My body shuddered as silent, hollow tears rattled free from my chest as the truth set in – I had run out of options. I took the briefest moment to appreciate the bitter September wind that crawled through the little window and nipped my face with night-frost. At least it was one small confirmation I was still alive, at least for the moment.

But that momentary relief was soon cut short as my senses began to focus and I heard … nothing. Not a single noise crept out of the Pines, out of the forest that had been chattering with the ominous sounds of wild-life mere minutes before. It had all fallen still, as if nothing at all existed in the blackness beyond the diner's neon domain. Earlier, I had feared those noises that lurked in the brush, but now all I wanted was to hear the owls on the wind one more time – just to prove I wasn't alone.

Tap tap tap. A soft tapping reverberated through the bathroom, pulling my attention away from the window. I listened intently, but I soon realized that the tapping wasn't coming from outside the bathroom as I had feared … it was coming from inside the bathroom itself, only feet away from where I was standing. I followed the taps like a bat follows its echoes until I found myself in front of the sink, face to face with the weathered mirror. But when I locked eyes with my reflection, I realized that mine was not the only mirrored the glass!

Next to my reflection stood the Piney, his gnarled finger tap-tap-tap-ping on the inside of the mirror, and behind him were dozens more people – men, women, children, young, old – all ethereal, their features clouded by the fogged glass. I even thought I caught a glimpse of the old man and the varsity jacket girl among their ranks, but I couldn't be sure. A legion of ghosts, if you'd call them that – the echoes of countless other travelers that had taken refuge at the Railyard Diner and paid the price. Just like me.

I saw the phantoms' mouths move, but no noise escaped their glass prison, save for only the tapping of the Piney's finger. Even though I couldn't hear them, I knew there was something they were trying to tell me, something important. The Piney's eyes were locked on the spot where his finger tapped again and again, as if telling me *"Here! Look here!"*

I followed his stained finger, my eyes focusing on a bit of scratched graffiti – at first glance, the etchings seemed like nonsense, but as I leaned my face closer to the glass, I realized that the scratch marks were words – but written backwards, scratched from inside of the mirror.

"W…O…N…T…U…O…T…E…G," I deciphered the words backwards, unscrambling the letters into a scrawled warning: *GET OUT NOW*.

"It's a little late for that," I scoffed to myself, my throat too barren to issue more than a dry wheeze in place of a laugh. But when my eyes turned back to the Piney, I saw him frantically scratching another message on his side of the glass, so desperate to communicate that he was scratching into the mirror with his own fingernails.

I watched in anticipation as each jagged letter came to life: "D…N…I…H…E…B". As my brain processed the message, my lips silently formed the word – *BEHIND*.

My heart froze solid. The ghostly captives were no longer looking at me… they were looking past me. The only reflection that still had its eyes on me was a stout old woman in a white collared shirt – Nora. And unlike the other ghosts, her reflection was partially obscured by my shoulder… because she was in the bathroom with me.

"Now what's all this fuss about?" Nora cooed as I spun on my heels, my heartbeat pounding in the recesses of my skull, growing louder and louder until I almost thought it would drone out even Nora's voice. The bathroom door was still closed, the knob still locked, the trash can unmoved – I had no idea how she made it inside. The old woman's withered mouth hung slightly ajar, as if she wanted to relish each morsel of fear in the air around us.

"You left in such a hurry," she frowned playfully, taking a step toward me, her lips curling backwards up her gray gums, revealing rows and rows of crooked, yellow-stained teeth that lined the inside of her vacuous mouth. Her gaze darkened, her pupils expanding until they devoured the whites of her eyes, leaving her with two black marbles focused squarely on me. "Did you even get a chance to look at the specials?"

Nora's spiderleg fingers crawled their way into her apron pocket, producing the specials menu that I had overlooked during my first visit. She looked down at the sheet, her grin growing unbearably twisted – when she looked back to me, her jaw crunched and snapped as it unhinged, opening wide like a serpent's maw to reveal the deep chasm of her monstrous throat.

"Oh look," she gurgled, "Today's special … is *you.*"

THE WIDOW &
THE RESURRECTION MAN

You know how much money you've got on you right now? Walking around with you, everywhere you go? All day, every day? It's worth more than you realize.

Not your wallet – Your heart. Your lungs. Your legs. Your liver. Your little finger. Your body, mate. Old thing's worth quite a lot to a guy like me.

That sounds more threatening than I meant it, but trust me, my living very much depends on your not continuing to do so. You've probably seen me before, but I doubt you noticed me – not really, anyhow. I don't stand out in a crowd. I'm dressed ordinary enough, lots of dark clothes – worn but not ratty – and a cap. Not one that'll attract any looks, you know, but something that keeps my eyes out of your sight.

Presentable, but never memorable – that's the trick.

I'm most often seen on a gray or gloomy day, but I don't bring the rains with me – or at least I don't mean to. It's just that folks always seem to die just in time to end up in the ground on the rainy days. But I don't mind – soggy rotten Massachusetts Sundays are just fine by me. Storms mean umbrellas, shorter ceremonies, people keeping their eyes down. Keeping their eyes off of me. And that suits me just fine.

I'll nod, but I won't ever speak to anyone. I'll lay flowers but I won't shake the widow's hand. They'll nod and say *'that you'* to no-one-in-particular, and that's how they'll remember me. A perfect nobody.

I make sure I pay my respects after of course – by that I mean I give a few dollars to the groundskeeper and the gravedigger, and maybe even drop some cash into the minister's personal coffer if he kept the rites short – and when everyone's grieved appropriately and the mourners head home, I stay behind for a few minutes, making a mental map of where this fresh resident has been put to rest amongst the city of crumbling headstones. I don't draw my routes on scraps of paper anymore – I used to, but if a cop catches you with a graveyard treasure map in your pocket, your whole operation is as good as blown. So keep it stored in your head, I say – keep it in the one place where only you can read it. And when your chips are down, just use those three magic words: *Deny, deny, deny.*

Later that night, once the sun has set and the clouds roll in from the sea to swallow the moon, I return to the graveyard gate that the groundskeeper has left unlocked, if he's made good on his word. If not, I know other ways to get in, but I'll break something on my way out for good measure, just to spite the old hypocrite.

I follow that map in my mind back through the maze of forgotten names and dates, past a stone cherub or two if the folks under my feet were fancy enough to afford such decorations, keeping myself low in the shadows until I finally return to that fresh patch of dirt.

That's when the shovel comes out.

If the gravedigger has held up his side of the silent bargain, the dirt has been laid in shallow and loose, so I won't be breaking my back unearthing the poor bastard from their dirt nap. If he's done his job, I'm down to the pine box in an hour and change. A crowbar takes care of the rest.

I pop the old boy open and the prize is waiting there for me – a perfect, quiet, well-dressed body just there for the taking. Some folks in my line of work operate in pairs, and that's probably smarter in the long run – that way you have someone to watch your back while you work, help you lift the heavier deadbeats. But I don't much care to split my earnings, so I make do with my own two hands.

Before I hoist the dead weight out of its snug resting place, I make sure to comb the stiff for any little baubles or jewels – a ring on the finger, a locket around the neck, a pocket watch tucked away in the folds of a vest. But don't misunderstand, I'm not some petty thief – I leave the shiny things behind in the casket. You see, cadaver jewelry is still considered family property, so you'll get slapped with jail time if they catch you trying to fence off some poor widower's rings, but in the eyes of the law, dead men's bones aren't anyone's property once they're in the ground. Long as I don't try to fleece any trinkets, *Wrongfully Disturbing a Corpse* is just a misdemeanor in the state of Massachusetts. Funny how that works, ain't it?

Besides, a pewter ring is chump change when compared to what I can get once I've lugged the corpse out of the dirt and onto my cart. I load my new silent friend onto the back of my wooden cart at the edge of the churchyard, cover the poor boy in fishing nets and blankets, and lead my donkey, Annie, down the cobblestone streets with steady steps. If I work quick, I'll make my exit around three in the morning, with only the streetlamps and the rats scurrying out of the sewer grates and the shadowed alleyways to see me go. Thankfully, my burro is a tough old girl, so those vermin don't spook her – even when rodents the size of alley cats skitter by as we stroll past the harbor.

At this time of night, in this sort of weather, chances are good that no one will bother me, but occasionally I get a few drunken stragglers or beguiled beggars crossing my path. A polite nod as I pass is usually enough to dissuade any unwanted attention, but my blood damn near curdled the other night when I ran headlong into a pair of coppers out on patrol:

The night was darker than most – roiling storms had rolled in from the Atlantic for the past week, which was useful for keeping prying eyes indoors, but it also meant that my typical excavation became an unwanted mud bath. So by the time I had slogged through the waterlogged grave and loaded the sodden dearly departed up onto Annie's cart, I was walking through the downpour wearing a contemptible glare and muck-caked trousers. Quite a sight, I'm sure.

As I turned the corner onto Charles Street, I nearly walked straight into a pair of silhouettes, shrouded beneath a market awning on this most auspicious night. When they stepped out of the darkness into the flickering lamplight, I could see the light glint off the corner of their chests – badges! Goddamn coppers…

At first, I tried to pass them by with a polite smile and a slight nod, hoping the rain would dissuade them from spending too much time on a nobody like me. I took a few more steps across the slick cobblestones before I heard a call from behind me, echoing over the growl of the rainfall:

"Oy!"

I cringed, my blood chilling, the patter of rain seeming to mock me for my hubris. But I knew I had no choice but to stop. Annie clopped to a halt and I took a few quick breaths to compose myself before the officers rounded the cart to reach me.

"Out late, ain't you, son," the first officer said as he looked me over, taking in every detail of my unimpressive appearance. His eyes were sunken into the shadows beneath his bobby hat and his expression was obscured by the matted mustache that consumed much of the officer's profile, rendering his face unreadable. Using my own tactics against me – *didn't he know that's cheating?*

"Aye, sir," I played along, keeping my gaze low behind the veil of the torrential downpour. "I wish I wasn't, but y'know, not much of a choice when the boss calls."

"Ain't that the truth," the second officer scoffed as he strolled past me and his compatriot. Uninterested in my tale of working-class woe, the tall officer instead spent his time investigating my cart. Annie was behaving herself – *good girl, don't give them a reason to look any closer.* A steadfast donkey can be the best of criminal cohorts.

"What did your boss have you coming out here so late for?" the mustached cop pressed, still suspicious. If I was him, I would be suspicious too.

"Captain wants me mending these nets," I quickly countered, bucking my head backwards towards the cart. "We've lost enough time as is with these storms keeping us in the harbor. Captain wants these nets ready to go the minute the clouds break so we can make the most of the halibut season before she's gone."

This was one of my pre-prepared stories, one of the half dozen excuses I kept loaded and ready to fire off at the first sign of trouble. I wasn't in the market to get pinned for brawling with a copper – not that I'd win against these two lugs anyhow – and in weather like this, I wasn't running anywhere, not that I'd dream of leaving poor Annie in the hands of the law. That meant talking my way out of this corner was my only option.

I was pretty sure I had the charm to reassure these oblivious officers, but if the tall one poked around the cart too much, he would unveil my lifeless cargo – and there's not enough gab in the world to bail me out of a pair of dead eyes looking up at him from a pile of fishing nets.

"Christ," the tall officer exclaimed when he reached the rear of my cart. "Smells awful back here!"

"Seaweed," I explained, keeping my composure as cool as the night wind. "When it starts to rot, the odor is something fierce. Like I said, these nets ain't seen salt water for days."

I shot an apologetic look over my shoulder at the tall officer, but the gruff lawman was too preoccupied gripping his nose to battle the death stench wafting off my cart. My expression remained friendly, but inside, clock hands were anxiously ticking – the longer I stood in this downpour, the more that body was going to bloat, soaking up the rainwater like a sponge. If I couldn't get moving soon, not only would I run the risk of being discovered but my cargo would be ruined. You can't make money off a misshapen stiff – they spoil, just like apples.

"I don't mean to be rude, sir," I began humbly, "but is there a reason you're stopping me? I've got a wife to keep fed at home and I can't afford to catch a chill out in this weather."

"We're stopping anyone out on the roads tonight," the mustached officer explained, clearly no more enthused to be out in this storm than I was, "Them gang kids – the Roxbury Rollers – they've been coming down harborways to make trouble lately, so we've got to check folks to make sure they're not doing something they shouldn't."

"Of course," I agreed in a barely-audible murmur. My prodding hadn't worked – my fate was out of my hands now.

"Oy!" the looming copper called out from behind the cart, startled by something I couldn't see. My frigid skin bristled and my hand wrapped around a razor tucked inside my long coat pocket, ready to slash at the mustached officer and make a mad dash towards the closest alley if the tall one unearthed my dead cargo from beneath its nautical camouflage. "Something's moving back here!"

"What sort of something?" the mustached copper called back, keeping his shadowed eyes fixed on me, waiting for some facial tick that would fly a guilty flag over my entire charade.

"Something you want to tell me, son?" the officer pried like a stern father with concern in his voice but a belt in his hand. I couldn't answer, unable to take my mind off the image of an ashen, blue-veined arm limply flopping free from beneath my nets.

The tall officer slowly pulled his nightstick from his belt loop, his intent stare never shifting from the serpentine mass of netting. He had seen some shuffle of movement, or at least thought he had. He cautiously prodded the pile of nets with his baton, seconds away from lifting the ropes … but just before he could, an engorged rat leapt from beneath the nets, hissing through gnarled yellow teeth before scurrying away into the deplorable night!

"GAH!" the tall officer hollered, dropping his nightstick and stumbling backwards as the rat slipped between his boots and off into the shadows. The officer turned his spooked eyes towards us, but quickly tried to compose himself, embarrassed by the schoolgirl cry that had just escaped his throat.

"Something the matter, sir?" I asked, innocent as a lamb, hoping to catch the officer on his back foot.

"Nothing, nothing…" the tall officer grumbled, quickly averting his eyes. "Just some big bastard rat. Thing ran off with a chunk of old fish from the nets."

"All the more reason I gotta clean and mend 'em," I agreed, pushing my advantage. After another few moments of grumbling between themselves, the mustached officer turned to me, shaking a flow of rain from his cap brim.

"Well, get along then, son," the officer said, cocking his head down the boulevard. "But make it quick and get on out of this rain – even on a night like this, there's bad folk about."

"Aye, sir," I nodded, tipping my cap to the lawman and guiding Annie down the street. The coppers returned to their post beneath the storefront canopy by the time I had reached the next corner and I quickly ducked my cart down an alleyway and out of sight.

When I checked the cargo, I was stunned to discover that it had not been a chunk of fish that the monstrous rat had in its teeth when it scurried off between the copper's legs – it had been one of my corpse's pinkie fingers! I'll admit… I laughed.

The rest of my nighttime excursion went uninterrupted – I stayed off the main roads in case the cops had other checkpoints along my way, finally emerging from the maze of back alleys at my destination: a nondescript iron gate, leading to the rear courtyard of a hospital that will remain unnamed – I need to preserve my professional integrity, of course.

At the base of the gate was a rain-spattered brass lantern, tucked behind one of the hospital's decorative bushes. I bent down and picked up the lantern, wiping away as much water as my soaked sleeve would accept. Drying my fingers as best I could, I lit a match from the recesses of my overcoat, igniting the lantern's oil. I then turned the flickering flame towards the hospital's basement window, which was barely visible between the bricks of the building's base – unless of course, you knew where to look.

Aiming at the slender window, I covered and uncovered the lantern glass in a series of three – *light, dark, light, dark, light, dark* – before extinguishing the flame with a swift puff of air from my tight lips. Then, I waited.

For a few interminable moments, I waited in the darkness of the hospital's looming shadow, not daring to ignite the lamp a second time. Thankfully, I finally spotted movement in the basement window and soon, a lit candle was placed on the windowsill – the cue I had been waiting for. I pushed the gate and it freely swung open on its wrought iron hinges, its lock lying in the grass a few feet away, unused. I guided Annie inside, keeping the jangling of her reins to a minimum until I reached the stairs leading down to the subterranean basement door – the unholy portal down into the hospital's subterranean morgue.

With a heavy *ker-chunk*, the basement's weighty deadbolt slid open and the thick wooden door soon followed suit, revealing a man in a white coat on the other side of the entryway.

"Come on," the doctor beckoned to me. "Bring your friend."

I did as I was told, tying up Annie beneath one of the courtyard's trees before lugging the stiff out of the cart and down the stone steps. I always groaned about the doctor not lending a hand with this exhausting descent, but the old man always replied with moans about professional integrity and not wanting to be seen. So I did as I was told.

After I finally slung the corpse onto a mental gurney at the bottom of the stairs, the doctor and I emerged from the shadowed tunnel into the dimly lit morgue. Firelight flickered across our faces and glinted in the dead man's glassy eyes, giving our trio the look of some profane creatures from the depths. I could see the doc's face better in the candlelight, his jagged silver eyebrows extenuating his pensive green eyes as shadows danced across his wizened face.

I had been working with Doc Sampson for more than a year and he had always been a trustworthy source of income – he was one of the leading surgeons in all of New England and I'm told he was once quite a star in the operating theaters of London and Paris during his time abroad. To hone his skills, he did what many other doctors and medical students were apt to do these days – purchase corpses for practice and experimentation, through entrepreneurs like me.

Doc Sampson was always adamant that his purchases were purely for the purposes of "medical advancement", but I didn't much care what he was doing with the stiffs once he handed over the money he owed me. Don't get me wrong, I liked the good doctor just fine – but this is a business to me, and the bottom line comes first.

Sampson told me random, rambling hospital tales as he ran his hands up and down the corpse, examining each joint and purple bruise to appraise the worth of this particular specimen. His stories were always interesting, if half-remembered, pulled from his trips overseas or maybe from a particularly rude patient from the day's operations. For this body, Sampson paid me forty dollars for my troubles, forgiving the rat-gnawed pinky finger but admitting that the rain-bloat had spoiled the corpse somewhat. That was fair, and forty dollars was more than enough to get me by until my next job.

I'm sure that you're looking at me with judgment in your eyes, reading about how casually I sell off my fellow man for a few bucks – but get those sorts of thoughts out of your head before you hurt yourself scowling. I don't have any guilt about what I do because most of you don't have any guilt when it comes to leaving your loved ones to rot.

Of all the stiffs I've pinched, I would say that a good three quarters of them wouldn't have seen any visitors within a year or two anyway. And when the dirt's replaced and the flowers are put back, who's going to know the difference? You've still got a headstone, you've still got your prayers if you can find the time for that sort of thing – but that body's as good as worm food as far as anyone but me is concerned.

You can call me a 'body snatcher' or a 'grave robber' or some morbid thing like that – and you'd be right. But personally, I prefer the name that Doc Sampson told me the Brits use for people like me – *a resurrection man*. I quite like the sound of that. Sophisticated like.

But after what I've seen in the last few days, I'm starting to regret that name.

Things started going wrong a week ago. Cops had started tightening patrols over the last few months – warmer time of year, more crime, more cops on the street. Unable to work in my usual way, I took a daytime job at a cobbler's shop, tanning and cleaning leather for a bespectacled Polish immigrant in the North End. It was honest work, but cutting cowhide was pennies compared to the money I usually made during the autumn resurrection season.

After a few weeks of biding my time, I finally decided to take the risk and commandeer the corpse of a young widow I had read about in the *Herald's* obituary page. The article said she had passed away during childbirth – the child survived, ending up in some orphanage no doubt. Without any family to claim the body, she was laid to rest at a potter's field in a pauper's grave – which meant shallow coffins and easy pickings.

I slipped the groundskeeper a few dollars to buy his preoccupation for a few hours, though my financial straits meant I couldn't pay the man as much as I would've liked. I'd have to work fast, in case the workman changed his mind and decided my bribe was too cheap to buy his silence. I dug in haste – thankfully, it was a dry night, so I was able to unearth the cheap pine casket with little fuss – though the crooked oak tree that towered above the widow's grave was casting queer, snaking shadows across the plot as I worked, leaving me uneasy and feeling as if I was trapped in the clutches of some great tentacled thing.

Soon, I was able to part the box from its dirt blanket and took to its nails with my crowbar, cracking the wood as I pried its lid free. Underneath the lid laid an elegant young woman, dressed in a lily-white muslin gown, her pale, pretty face preserved in a peaceful expression – quite the opposite of the painful death she surely endured. She had been a woman that would've turned heads strolling past shop windows on Arlington Street or while sitting by the lapping banks of the Charles on some Spring day. Taken before her time – a shame, really. I tried to assure myself she'd be put to better use in Doc Sampson's hands.

I got to work, removing a few pieces of pauper's jewelry from her limp limbs – a brass bracelet, a dented wedding band. When I reached her chest, I found a turquoise brooch hanging from a thin silver chain around her neck, buried amongst the white folds of her dress – it was beautiful, shimmering wildly in the moonlight like polished tortoiseshell, made from some sort of sea crystal. A nice piece certainly, especially for a woman of her means – I would think to find such a brooch on the bejeweled neck of some socialite or high-class heiress. My guess was that it had been a family heirloom, perhaps from her mother's mother in more prosperous times.

I knew my rules, and I stuck to them religiously on every other job I had pulled as a resurrectionist – but for whatever reason, I couldn't pry my eyes away from that glinting brooch. I couldn't bear to leave it in that pine box beneath the ground, never to catch the moonlight through its prism again. I'm not one for trinkets, but a whisper in the back of my mind hissed, *"Take it. No one will know."*

So I did.

I unclasped the chain from around her cold throat as gingerly as I could manage and slipped the broach into my coat pocket – then, after a few seconds, I moved it into my inner breast pocket. I didn't want to risk dropping it… parting with it. After my spoils were amply secured, I loaded the thin widow's body onto Annie's cart, her waifish figure making this cargo considerably easier to lug out of the graveyard.

Annie's hooves clacked down the cobblestones in the sticky late-summer night, but thankfully, we remained unnoticed by the sleepy populace that had been lulled into a deep, sweaty slumber by the overbearing humidity. A gang of school-age children crossed our path while darting between back alleys, but we suffered no more than a few schoolyard jeers – though I thought I felt the broach jostle in my pocket as they passed.

Finally, we arrived at the back gate of Sampson's hospital, but my skeleton nearly jumped from my skin when I peered through the wrought iron gate and saw one of the hospital orderlies standing in the middle of the courtyard, puffing away on a crumpled cigarette! I tried to leap back out of sight, but I was too late – the man in the white scrubs spotted me and barked out from across the clearing:

"Hey! What's it you're doing there?"

"Evenin there, sir," I quickly composed myself, bowing my head as a courtesy, but moreso to keep the orderly's gaze off my face. "Just passin' through with my wares! Could I offer you some fresh produce or the like?"

The orderly scoffed and stamped out the embers of his cigarette, thin wafts of smoke billowing out from beneath his boot heel. Seeing little importance in some gutter merchant like me, he averted his eyes with a disinterested scoff.

"Ah go peddle somewhere else," he grumbled. "What kind of damned fool tries to sell fruit at a goddamn hospital, at this time of night? A right idiot, if you ask me…"

"Aye sir, a right idiot indeed," I nodded without a second glance, taking Annie by the reins and guiding her out of sight of the black infirmary gates. I hoped to all hope that my late-night excursion wouldn't be enough to make me memorable in the mind of this brutish orderly – if he reported me for 'suspicious goings-on', I'd be forced to find a new buyer for my particular sort of cargo, and that was far easier said than done. There aren't any want ads in the trades for folks of my skill set, that I can assure you.

I circled the neighborhood for another quarter of an hour before returning to the back gate, keeping Annie out of sight while I scoped for danger – thankfully, the orderly had returned to his post inside and the courtyard was again left shadowed and abandoned. Just how I liked it.

I flashed my lantern signal and soon received a response – I hitched Annie in the alleyway outside, now paranoid that the orderly would glance out the window and see the silhouette of our cumbersome cart. Instead, I rolled the widow's body up in an old tarp I kept folded in the cart-bed and draped the woman over my shoulder, carrying her across the courtyard as casually as if I was delivering a carpet to some housewife.

Thankfully, Sampson was quick with the door, so I wasn't forced to spend too much time vulnerable out in the open. Once deep inside the morgue, I gently laid the widow down on a shining gurney and unrolled her fabric shell, as if unveiling some great treasure.

"Oh my," Sampson mulled in that cryptic way he always spoke. Always brewing, always calculating. "Quite the specimen you've brought me."

"I aim to please, Doc," I shrugged, leaning against the wall and beginning to roll a cigarette – the orderly had planted the idea in my head and now I was craving a smoke myself.

"Do not do that in here, please," Sampson remarked without taking his eyes off the body as he performed his routine examination, as if he could sense the tobacco's presence in his sanitized temple of cleanliness.

"Just rolling, Doc, just rolling," I mumbled before slipping the half-packed cigarette back into my pocket, my fingers brushing across the smooth edges of the brooch, sending a warm sensation through me. I had never owned something so nice, not really.

"How old is this one?" Sampson asked while he lifted the arm, checking the rigor mortis in the widow's joints.

"Twenty-four, I think," I replied, trying to remember the dates that had been printed in the obituary. As my eyes drifted down her slender, silent form, I noticed a concave crevice that ran down her abdomen, shrouded by her thin muslin gown – they had cut her open while she was still alive. Poor girl. "She had just given birth."

"Very well," Sampson remarked, slipping his half-moon spectacles off his nose. "She'll be a perfect subject for my next round of testing – the doctors of Massachusetts are shockingly uneducated when it comes to female physiology, especially during pregnancy. This young lady will help us to bridge that gap."

Sampson reached into his coat pocket and handed me a bundle of bills, adding a few more on top for good measure. When I counted the bounty, it totaled seventy dollars – more than I had ever been paid for a single stiff in all my time as a resurrection man in the Doc's employ.

"Now, if you'd be so kind," Doc Sampson motioned towards a wall of square metal doors. They were massive sliding drawers, used for storing the Doc's bodies. I nodded, stripping out of my coat as the Doc unlocked one of the chest-level drawers and slid the slab forward – we then took either end of the widow's body and lowered her onto the chilly metal box, rolled the body deep into the shadows, and latched the drawer shut. This part of the operation always struck me with a tinge of melancholy – the stiffs I brought to Doc Sampson were just trading one pitch black tomb for another.

"I can see myself out," I shrugged when Sampson offered to walk me to the door. As I flung my coat back over my shoulders, the brooch came tumbling out of my pocket and clattered across the slick morgue floor. My eyes shot to the necklace, my heart dropping, unsure if Doc Sampson would be angry that I pinched something from the poor widow's casket, or worse yet, if he would claim it for his own – but the old doctor clocked the concern in my gaze before I could explain.

"Risky, no? Taking trophies," he asked benignly as I scampered to pick the turquoise stone up off the ground, shoving the necklace back into my pocket. I didn't answer him. "Ah, it's your business, after all. Do what you like – just keep yourself out of trouble."

"Sure," I murmured, my mind unable to focus on anything but the broach now pressed against my breast, only a thin strip of vest fabric separating my bare skin from its touch. Just as I raised my fingers to caress its crystal creases – *BANG!*

Doc Sampson and I leapt at the sudden slamming sound, though we could not identify its source for the life of us. But the noise didn't leave us wondering for long –

BANG! It went again, this time the sound reverberating with a distinctly metallic sound – it was coming from the wall of corpse drawers.

"It is probably the summer heat… warping the metal," Doc Sampson guessed, though there was little in his voice to assure me of his confidence. "It will soon settle."

As if issuing a spiteful reply, slamming came again from the wall of metal caskets – *BANG! BANG! BANG!* With this violent volley, it was made very clear to us where the frantic disturbance was coming from: the very same drawer we had just used to seal the widow away.

"Did you bring me a –?" Sampson began to ask, befuddled.

"I didn't bring you no breather!" I hissed back, insulted by the insinuation. I was a professional, goddamn it – I would never have made such a greenhorn mistake.

Sampson began to walk towards the widow's compartment, inching closer, body tense in anticipation for the next slam. I didn't dare take another step closer – I had handed over the body; whatever was happening now wasn't part of my job description. I felt my fingers crawl their way into my pocket, gripping the brooch for protection.

With a ginger hand, Sampson slowly unlatched the compartment door and cautiously opened the mouth of the metal tunnel, its contents shrouded in lightless shadow. The only thing visible in the blackness was a few golden strands of the widow's hair, splayed out like a spiderweb from the crown of her unseen head. Almost too petrified to go further, the good doctor finally wrapped his thin fingers around the end of the cadaver slab and rolled the corpse out into the open to find … nothing.

Nothing was out of place, nothing had changed. The beautiful widow's body still lay stiff and unmoving, her ashen arms still by her side. The inside of the metal door was free from dents or palm prints and the slamming had fallen mercifully silent.

"You must've been right, Doc," I chuckled dryly, my heart nearly beating through my ribcage. "Heat's gone and done it."

"Yes, I suppose it must have…" the doctor nodded, still perplexed by the strange scene. I had no desire to stick around for another round of bizarre goings-on, so I took this lull in excitement to see myself out through the morgue's rear tunnel. When I emerged out into the courtyard, I lit my crooked cigarette and tried to ignore how the match quivered in my hands.

When I inhaled, the smoke tasted putrid. I stomped it out and walked Annie home.

I slept through most of the next day, as I often do after a long night of work, but this time I stained my rickety flophouse bed with sweat as I tossed and turned in the sweltering summer heat that crept into my room through the cracks in the walls.

But it wasn't just the heat that brought on my sweats – for hours I dreamt fractured, wild dreams; I felt like I was falling through an endless black pit, surrounded by shapes and creatures I couldn't even begin to describe, terrified to think of what I'd find when I eventually hit the inevitable bottom. But that bottom never came – just the spiraling glare of eyes without a body, the moanings of a mind without a brain.

It must have been hours into my tumultuous slumber when she appeared – the face of the widow from the potter's field. Her gray eyes were the first to emerge from the darkness, staring at me though I had no form in my dream. The rest of her pale face soon appeared from the void, like she was surfacing from beneath some black lake. For a moment, there was peace between us as her vacant, angelic face floated mere inches from mine – but then, her graceful features began to change – to rot!

Her mouth turned to a devilish grimace as her lips shriveled and pulled away from her teeth, her cheeks hollowing as decay devoured her porcelain skin! Her strands of flaxen blonde hair turned brittle and disintegrated into horrid dust as her nose melted free from her skull and plunged down deeper into the blackness. Her eyes were the last to go, never blinking, never averting their piercing gaze, even as they withered inside her sockets like dried grapes and rolled away into the ether! All that remained was the widow's yellowed, screaming skull – and the brooch, glinting with its teal brilliance in the skull's left socket.

The skull spoke to me, but its voice echoed like a voice calling from the depths on a mineshaft, an unintelligible echo alien to human ears. Before I could decipher the widow's words, the skull roared forward with a banshee screech, violently tearing me from my slumber and launching me straight up on my sweat-stained mattress!

I haven't slept much since that first morning.

Over the next couple of days, I tried my best to return to my normal routine – I went back to my job at the cobbler, though with the roll of bills that Sampson had handed me, I didn't have much immediate need for money. But I returned nonetheless, to keep up appearances.

Two days after my dream, I started to see her on the street. I saw the flapping tail of a muslin gown amongst the countless legs of pedestrians, the cloth untouched by the street mud as it flowed regally over the cobblestones. I would see billows of flaxen hair dancing from around a street corner, then again from behind a newspaper stand or a rolling carriage two blocks later. It was rare that I would glimpse her face in these fleeting moments, but whenever I was unlucky enough to do so, I would always find her gray eyes glaring back, unnoticed by anyone else on the street, save for me. Whenever she was around, the brooch felt heavier in my pocket – sometimes that was all the indication I needed to know she was watching me.

"I'll sell it off soon," I repeated to myself again and again. "I just need to find someone who'll fence it for me." But I didn't sell it – I soon found myself wearing it by the silver chain around my neck. For safekeeping.

By the third day, I had stopped sleeping altogether – I couldn't bear the torment of that skull again. Hell, it had burnt itself into my mind so thoroughly I could've sworn I would sometimes see its grotesque grimace for just a second when I closed my eyes, even when awake. The cobbler mentioned that I looked haggard, and he was right – my eyes were crimson and sunken into my head, my skin was yellowed and greasy, my hair unkempt. I was looking worse by the hour, but what choice did I have? The closest thing I found to salvation was the moments when I'd lay on my bed, trying to rest without allowing myself to drift into full sleep – into her domain – while clutching the brooch tight between my fingers.

As the days dragged on, my condition continued to spiral further and further downward until finally reaching the pit's dark bottom. When returning from the cobbler's shop earlier tonight, I came back to my flop-house room to find my door ajar. I froze feet from the threshold, unable to bring myself to find out what was waiting for me on the other side. Through the crack between the doorframe, I saw something shift in the blue moonlight that spilled across the mismatched wooden floorboards – a shadow, a wisp of cloth, billowing in the night air. It was her – the widow – she had finally followed me home, to claim my soul or whatever it was that her dead mind was hell bent on achieving!

But knowing I had nowhere else to run, I finally found motion in my feet and moved towards my room, the door screeching as it swung open on its warped hinges. I stepped through the entryway, bracing myself for what-ever horror awaited me on the other side, but when I finally peered through squinting eyelids, I found a far more tangible threat – I had been robbed.

My room was in a horrible state of disrepair – clothing strewn across the floor, bed upended, cabinets torn from their places and scattered around the room – a right ransacking if I'd ever seen one. When I checked the door, I realized that in my sleep-deprived state, I must've forgotten to latch the lock when I left that morning, leaving me vulnerable to wandering hands – though I could not shake the feeling that the widow had somehow played a part in this new misfortune. Whatever the cause, ghostly or not, my money was gone. The burglars had taken anything with the slightest value, leaving me penniless, save for the few dollars I had in my pocket and the brooch that still hung from around my neck. Sampson's payment was gone, and with it went my ability to pay my rent, due at the end of the week.

If I wanted to hold on to my little corner of the flophouse and keep out of debtor's jail, I only had one option left – harvesting headstones.

So, like a bat returning to the familiar recesses of its dark cave, I slunk back to the graveyard that night beneath the cover of the dusk shadows. The few crumpled dollars in my back pocket wouldn't be enough to buy

me a kick in the ass from the groundskeeper, much less a few hours of solitude, so I would have to return to my body snatching roots and perform
this job pro-bono. This particular graveplot's guardian took a break to grab
a pint at a nearby pub around ten in the evening, so I bided my time until
the gruff groundskeeper took his leave and I slipped through a gap in the
southern corner of the churchyard fence. It was a tight fit – I'd have to find
another way out when I returned with my cargo – but for now, everything
was going according to plan.

I jogged between headstones, looking for signs of new burial –
if the grave had grass, I wasn't interested. I didn't have the time – the
groundskeeper's bar outing would only buy me forty minutes, an hour
tops. So, when I finally came across the grave of a recently interred sailor, I
got to work. Dirt flew into the night as I dug deep – I didn't pay any mind
to the mess. Speed was my only mission. With each strike of my shovel, I
felt the brooch jostle beneath my shirt, its presence giving me the strength
to continue my mad excavation.

Finally, caked with dirt and worm-rot, I struck wood – the sailor's
casket! My hands flew with frenzied energy to pry the lid open, as if feeling the groundskeeper's breath down my neck as I scrambled to free the
corpse from its ditch. I finally ripped the lid free, revealing the gnarled stiff
inside, his tattoos still visible on the death-dried skin beneath his sailor's
uniform. I would've given a salute if I had the time. But just as I reached
down to pull the sailor out of his pine box, I felt the brooch run cold against
my skin and suddenly the sailor grabbed my wrist!

At first, I thought the corpse's arm had just clattered its way onto
me, but when I tried to pull back, I found the skeletal fingers tightened
around my flesh, holding me close in the grave pit. The body's rigor mortis
strength kept me trapped despite my resistance, and as I leaned in closer
to try to gain some leverage, the sailor's dead jaw groaned open and words
escaped its haunted throat:

"*T h i e f,*" the body moaned, its jaw cracking open wide, as if trying to swallow me whole! My fear finally granted me the strength to wrench myself free, ripping myself away from the sailor and taking his arm with me! As I struggled to pry myself free from the arm's disembodied grip, the sailor's corpse sat straight up, its vacant sockets targeting me:

"*Thiiiiieeeeffffff,*" the sailor bellowed in a voice like air gurgling up from a pit of sea muck as it pulled itself up onto its stiff feet and stomped toward me. The sailor's remaining limbs clung to its fraying sinew as the body rose, its rotted eyes glowing a sickening azure green as it shuffled towards me.

"Get back!" I yelled, my sleep-deprived brain accepting whatever I was seeing as fact. I grabbed one of the casket's wooden planks and held it like a club, ready to strike the corpse as it trudged towards me. The creature took no notice of my warnings and I struck it across the head with the plank, shattering a section of skullbone like a piece of old pottery! But my strike did little to dissuade the sailor's approach. Its glowing eyes grew closer and closer as the rancid soup that had once been the seaman's brains leaked from the hole in its temple...

"Damn you!" I cried, charging the walking corpse with the plank, stabbing it through the torso and pinning it to the earthen wall of the grave ditch. The remains of the sailor's muscles kept the body pinned to the soil wall as I backed away, the reanimated corpse never showing signs of pain, never slowing its efforts as it clawed at the air, trying to force its way towards the fleshier parts of my body.

I pulled myself from the ditch, trying in vain to catch my breath and steady my stomach after such a supernatural assault, the brooch pressed against my skin with an unearthly chill. But on a night like tonight, it seemed peace was not an option.

As I gazed in horror around the churchyard, all of the surrounding graves were shaking in the moonlight, their soil mounds quaking as the corpses beneath rebelled against their man-made confinement. The grave-yard residents were waking, all hell-bent on reaching me!

Without a second thought, I turned on my heels and sprinted towards the crooked portion of fence through which I had entered, trying hard to ignore the groans of the undead that now clawed at my heels from beneath their earthen resting places. I squeezed through the gap in the bent iron bars and burst out onto the street, the bemoaned cries of those ghouls echoing through my ears like a symphony of terror.

I didn't delay – thankfully, I knew that an operation as covert as this meant leaving Annie at home, so the poor girl wasn't accosted by the phan-toms that now assaulted my senses. I ran from the graveyard, my fright propelling my limbs and sending me stumbling down the cobblestone boulevards, running from that cursed plot. However, the spirits' whispers wouldn't leave my skull as I careened down the alleyways, trying to lose the phantasms in the maze-like side streets of Boston.

Finally, I crashed into the black iron gates of Sampson's hospital, my legs nearly giving out from beneath me as shock pushed my body to its physical and mental limits. I pulled on the gates, but I soon realized they were locked – when preparing for my last-minute mission, I had forgotten to give Sampson notice that I would be coming, so the courtyard had not been prepared for my arrival. I could feel the phantom screams barreling down on me, and worrying what would happen if those ethereal voices were to reach me, I used my frantic strength to pull myself over the hospi-tal gate and crash onto the courtyard cobblestones below.

My shoulder screamed as I pulled myself up off the frigid stone, clawing my way towards the basement steps. I think I broke something in that fall… But I didn't have time to worry about that injury now – not while my mortal soul was at stake. I slammed into the heavy wooden door, anticipating the resistance of an iron latch lock – but when I made impact, the door swung open freely. I was taken aback by the easy entry and proceeded down the morgue tunnel as cautiously as my frayed nerves could muster.

I limped down the tunnel, holding myself up with a shaky hand against the wall, leaving a trail of cold sweat behind me as I descended deeper into the morgue. One oil lamp flickered next to Doc Sampson's desk in the corner, dancing a weak flame across the shadowed examination tables as the rest of the cold room remained bathed in darkness.

"Doc?" I whispered, worrying that the dead would hear me if I spoke too loud. There was no candle in the window, but the oil lamp by the desk gave me hope that the good doctor was taking care of some late-night work. I'm not a smart man by any means, so if anyone would know what to do, it would be Doc Sampson.

"Doc! You here?" I hissed through my teeth. "Something's going on… something's after me! You gotta hide me!"

I reached Doc's desk and snatched the oil lamp, trying to cast away the blackness of the hospital's basement in search of the old man. At first, there was nothing – no doctor, no ghouls, no noise save for the moaning of the harbor winds outside. But as I swung the lamplight across the subterranean room, the breath was ripped from my lungs in silent fright.

As the orange flame danced across the rows of polished metal cadaver drawers, they glimmered in the darkness like bared animal teeth – but I soon found a gap in the twisted smile. One of the drawers was open. When I looked at the small gold numbering above its unlocked door, I realized that this was the same compartment where we had entombed the widow's corpse just days prior. But the woman was gone … and at the foot of her former resting place, there was a body. Doc's body.

I scrambled with frantic energy to the good doctor's side – at first, I hoped that the old man had simply collapsed on the job, from exhaustion or a weak heart or something of the like. At least if that was the case, there was hope for Sampson – we were in the bowels of a hospital after all. But after the devilish sights I had already endured tonight, I had little faith in any easy explanation – and when I finally illuminated Sampson's body, my fears were realized:

Old Doc Sampson was lying in a pool of his own black blood, his limbs haphazardly flopped at his side at queer angles. The space between his forehead and his nose was completely caved in, to the point that his face was nigh-unrecognizable underneath the mounds of mangled flesh and shattered bone. That powerful brain of his was nothing more than corned beef now. Upon looking up to the glinting shelves, I saw the sleek metal door of the widow's drawer was riddled with dents and stained with flecks of dried blood – the vengeful thing had used the drawer handle to stove in the poor doctor's head with an ungodly fury.

Just then, I saw the blur of a white figure reflected in the distorted mirror of the dented door. She was in the room with me. Right behind me.

With all my options extinguished, I turned to face my waifish tormentor. There she was, standing, or perhaps hovering, with a silent grace, her hair floating as if floating beneath the waves of some gentle harbor, concealing her eyes from view. In that brief gasp of a moment, the widow looked like nothing more than a mournful young flower, wilted at the tips but still an elegant bulb. I could've run to her, embraced her, like a wounded thing to be cared for – but I knew her innocence was a smokescreen. I could still see Doc Sampson's blood caked underneath her cracked fingernails.

As if sensing her ruse had been discovered, the widow's head snapped up, her eyes crackling with the same haunting energy that had possessed the sailor and the other corpses – or perhaps they had all been the widow, her influence, all along. With a banshee screech ripped from my nightmares, the pale phantom flung herself towards me, murder in her glare!

I did the first thing that came to my mind, the only option I had left in my exhausted bag of tricks: I leapt inside the open cadaver drawer, using all my strength to slam the dented door closed behind me, locking myself in the near-perfect blackness of the metal casket! I had only a few inches of clearance between my trembling body and the cold container walls, but there was now a barrier between me and the widow and that's all that mattered for the moment.

But a thin metal latch door did not deter the widow's vengeance as she began to bang her fists against the drawer with hellish strength, deepening the already warped dents, pounding them closer to the crown of my head. It was during this siege that I reached beneath my shirt and felt the brooch – it was warm, its heat growing with every inch closer the widow drew. I rubbed my quaking fingers over the crystal slopes, but this time, the brooch brought me no comfort.

"Please!" I moaned, begging from inside my self-interred tomb. "It's just a necklace! Please, I didn't mean to–!"

BANG BANG BANG! My pleas fell upon dead ears.

"You didn't need it anymore! I couldn't just leave it," I justified. But my excuses did not impress my attacker. The banging continued, the door hinges beginning to whine as they held on for dear life. "All this for a bleeding brooch?!"

As I frantically passed the broach between my fingers, I felt my skin catch against a little latch on the necklace's side – a minute detail I hadn't noticed during my many hours wearing the stolen amulet. Clicking my nail against the tiny latch, I felt the brooch open, revealing its gem to be a hollow construction of simple sea glass, housing something else within.

Using my free hand to guide the broach to one of the few shafts of meager light that clawed through the dented drawer door, I carefully opened the necklace to reveal its mystery contents: inside, I found a short lock of curled brunette hair and a charcoal sketch of a baby girl, no larger than a penny. I was dumbfounded – of course! The widow's child! It was never about the brooch itself – the necklace was the last remnant of the widow's soul, the last scraps of her connection with the daughter she didn't live to see. And I had stolen it from her.

Possessed by a wave of overwhelming shame and a spark of tenderness, I knew what I had to do. Gingerly holding the lock of her daughter's hair in my palm, I release my grip on the dented door, knowing that the widow's cold whiteness awaits me on the other side.

I have nowhere else to run, no excuses left, no more feats of resurrection at my disposal. As I let this door creak open, my only hope now was forgiveness, and a mother's love...

MATCHSTICK

IT IS THE 18TH DAY OF SEPTEMBER, 1930 – it is harvest season in Yardley, Pennsylvania.

There is smoke in the air.

There's a fire on the Bankson homestead. Word spreads quickly between farms, passing from family to family as fast as each sprinting messenger's feet can take it. If the blaze spreads through Ed Bankson's property, it could take many more farms with it. The town moves as one, each family bringing whatever they can to combat the oncoming flames.

Your father wakes you from your bed – you are coming with him, to fight the blaze head on with the other farmers. Your mother and your sister are staying behind to protect the house in case the fire jumps fields while you and your father grab your heavy wool coats and run out into the crisp, crackling night. He stations you at the Bankson well and you run water buckets back and forth until the sun begins to pierce the bleak morning. But you're happy to do it. To take your first step towards becoming a Yardley Man.

When the embers finally heave their last gasps and extinguish, Ed Bankson's barn is nothing more than a charred skeleton in the gray morning mist. The field around it had also been left blackened, and much of his corn is smoldering and ruined – but thankfully, the swift efforts of the rest of you Yardley folk helped contain the blaze, sparing the rest of Bankson's harvest and his homestead, though the house siding was scorched by a few licks of flame.

However, when Ed Bankson finally takes stock of his property and his family, he makes a horrifying realization: he is missing a son. A search begins and you sift through cornstalks looking for the missing son – Ed's youngest, Joshua. But you don't find anything – it's Ned Kelly, the general store clerk, who yells from the ashen remains of the barn that he's found the boy.

Joshua's body is pinned under the charcoal remains of one of the barn rafters, burnt nearly beyond recognition. Near him are fire-warped oil tankards at the epicenter of the barn blaze. No one wants to say it, but a ripple of realization passes through the crowd – Joshua started the fire himself. But no one was about to say that to poor Ed's face. Your father leads you away, back across the fields to the weary arms of your mother. You did well.

You lay awake the next night, unable to sleep. The scent of charred wood still burns your nose, the glint of the little candle on your nightstand catches your wary eye as it sends long, crooked shadows dancing across your bare bedroom. It still doesn't make sense to you – you had known Joshua. He was a few years younger than you – three years junior to your mature old age of thirteen – but you had known Joshua long enough to know that he wasn't one of those firestarter kids that hang out by the general store, burning anthills with their father's glasses. He wasn't a troublemaker.

Maybe he had been playing around. Maybe it was an accident. It's possible, you think – Joshua is a silly kid.

W*as*. Was a silly kid, you remind yourself.

The Banksons hold a funeral for Joshua. You attend. Your mother bought your funeral suit for you three years ago, so the sleeves are already short on your wrists. There's talk that Ed and his family might up and leave Yardley – their crop is crippled, the grief, or maybe even the shame, might be too much for them to bear. People nod and say that they 'understand' – they won't blame Ed if that's what he feels he has to do. You don't want the Banksons to leave. It just wouldn't be fair.

Your mother brings you with her when she takes a parcel of food over to the Banksons. She gives Martha Bankson her deepest condolences and you echo her at a low mumble. At the doorway, you catch Joshua's sister looking at you, her eyes sunken and glassy with fear. You only knew Joshua from school, so you have never been introduced to his sister. She looks tired. Your mother leaves before you can say anything to the girl, but you give a timid wave as you depart. When you're halfway down the path, she waves back from the corner of her window.

You go back to school the next few weeks, and most everything returns to normal. You don't hear much from the Banksons anymore, but then again, no one does. You see Joshua's sister on the street every now and again and share a friendly smile, but you're always on errands, so you don't stop to talk. The skies darken, the wind whips and moans, laden with the sweet smells of tree sap, the changing leaves turning the forests on the edge of town into auburn infernos.

Autumn has come to Yardley, and with it, shadows.

When you're not in school or running errands for your mother, you help your father with chores around the farm – you're a man now, after all, and that comes with responsibilities. On a brisk Autumn morning, you carry a new sack of grain feed over to your family's cow pen, your shoulders growing taut and strong from years of farm work. The cows are happy to see you, greeting their next meal with a chorus of lazy moans and moos – however, one of the newborn calves in the middle of the herd catches your eye. The young animal sways unsteady on its feet, its eyes glazed over, its sweat-flecked body beset by a colony of buzzing flies. Its hind leg has turned a sickening shade of gray, scabbed over with layers of putrefaction and ichor puss.

You run to find your father, telling him that one of the newborns has come down with a case of black leg. You ask him what you should do to save the poor thing, but your father just sighs and purses the leathery skin of his brow between his sandstone fingers – "Ain't nothing to do but wait for it to die" is all he can muster.

With the rootworm blight that's been going around, the corn rust that killed Pete Freidkin's crop this summer… then the fires, and now this… you ask your father if Yardley's cursed like some of the other children say. You ask if it's time to leave, like so many other families already have.

"Our folk spent plenty of sweat and blood to make this patch of dirt ours," your father grimaces, greeting the cold air as it rustles through the corn stalks. "We ain't going anywhere."

The harvest festival is held at the end of September, on the night of the Autumn Equinox. The old midwife Clarissa Hartman calls it 'Mabon', but you don't know what she's talking about – no one really does. Every town has its own Clarissa Hartman. You feel the excitement in cool dusk air as you watch the tents being raised in the wide grass field behind the Presbyterian church; torches are lit and banners reading "Yardley Harvest Festival – 175 years" are hung. You help tie corn husks to the maypole at the center of the festival grounds. You wish you could be the one put the jack-o'-lantern in its place at the very top of the pole, but you know that's a privilege reserved for one of the older boys.

By the time the amber harvest moon looms massive in the sky, the festivities are in full swing and all of Yardley has come out to dance to music of the fiddle-and-washpan band and drink the fermented apple cider being tapped from a long row of chestnut casks. The flicker of firelight flirts with the waltz of the field's lighting bugs, painting the festival in a fairy glow.

When your head emerges from the chilly waters of the apple bobbing bucket, you see that even the Banksons have decided to come. Ed is still as gray as he was when you last saw him on that mournful day, now nearly a month ago, but Joshua's sister is standing off to the side of the bottle ring tent, wearing a necklace of warm orange leaves that bring light to her thin features.

You finally work up the courage and walk over to the Bankson girl, introducing yourself while barely taking your eyes off the buckles on your only pair of 'party shoes' – hand-me-downs, and what's more, they don't match. She smiles softly, her face partially sheltered by her cascade of wispy blonde hair. She introduces herself – her name is Kate.

From then forward, you and Kate are inseparable at the festival, your antics coaxing a stifled giggle or two from the shy farmgirl. While reaching for a candied apple from Clarissa Hartman's sweets stand, your hand brushes against Kate's delicate fingers – the autumn night air has left her with a freezing touch, but you find yourself warmed by her nonetheless.

As the festival grows long and raucous and the mulled cider beginning to take a hold of its warm-blooded hosts, the Banksons decide to leave, Kate following reluctantly behind them. You promise you will see her later, and even consider leaving your friends at the festival to chase after her – after all, the Bankson farm is only a few fields away from yours – but before you can give the idea much though, the wild fiddle-playing is abruptly cut short.

The pastor yells to the crowd that the Janie family's homestead is up in a blaze! All the drunken crowd needs to see is the crackling glow of the flames over the tree line to sober up and burst into action.

When the town arrives to battle the fire, you realize that this blaze is far more vicious than the Bankson fire – Hank Janie was one of the only men in town who owned a car, and by the time you get there, you find the jalopy engulfed in a sea of flame that has already crawled across the Janies' lawn and clawed its way up the side of their farmhouse. Against the blackness of the Equinox night, the fire in the farmhouse's windows gives the burning building the appearance of some great dead skull, its blazing eyes staring straight through you.

As men throw buckets of dirt and water atop what parts of the inferno they can reach, a scream pierces the night, battling its way past the fire's roar to be heard. The Janies are still inside! But the fire radiates such a powerful ring of scorching heat that you don't dare step closer, and you see many of the adults feel the same way. As the cries grow hoarse and even more panicked, you watch your father charge towards the burning farmhouse, armed only with the weathered longcoat on his back, and smashes through the front door, disappearing into the great skull's flaming maw.

After interminable minutes of waiting, punctuated by a few grating coughs from within the veil of black smoke, your father finally comes bursting out of the groaning husk with Ma Janie and Jess Janie under his arms, their faces soot-caked and their legs weak. All three collapse at your feet, the mother and daughter holding tight to each other as they expel coal miner coughs from their petite lungs. You quickly kneel to help your father pat away the few tongues of flame that cling to his coat, but you don't dare to look too long at his his face – his mad dash had left him scorched and blistered, his entire body stained by the nauseating smell of toasted flesh.

When your father is once again able to stand, he announces to the crowd that Hank Janie is dead – he saw his charred corpse amongst the flaming furniture of the kitchen. There's no hope for him. But he had not found the Janies' last daughter, Anabelle – news that send Ma Janie into a state of choked hysterics.

"Look! In the window!" you hear yourself yell over the commotion of the hopeless adults. You would never have spoken out like that on your own, but when you turned your eyes up to one of the farmhouse's glinting windows and saw the face of Annabelle Janie staring back down at you, a force seized you. There was no time for shyness, not now.

Following your finger, the crowd erupts into hollers upon seeing the girl's face looking out from the smoking bedroom. They call to Anabelle, begging her to open the window or smash the glass – if she can jump out the window, they can catch her! Even you offer your twig-skinny arms as reinforcements, but Anabelle does not move an inch – her eyes stare straight at the crowd, but register nothing, her blank expression never shifting even as the fire begins to consume the room behind her.

Ma Janie wails up to Anabelle, telling her not to be scared and to jump, but you don't think she's scared at all. Anabelle gives one more disinterested look out to the crowd before slowly retreating away from the window and into the arms of the flaming bedroom behind her. The smoke fogs the glass, so you're not able to see what happens in those final moments, but when the farmhouse collapses in on itself seconds later, Anabelle's fate is made certain.

There is another funeral. Another time of mourning. But this time, the surviving Janies don't stick around. Off to Pittsburg was the story, but people aren't really sure. One morning, the Janies were just gone.

Your father guesses at the cause of the Janies' fire – "that damned contraption sprung a leak", he grumbles in reference to Hank's car. But even a man as distrusting of automobiles as your father admits that he doesn't know how the automobile's fuel was set aflame to start the whole disaster into motion. After a few more silent moments of deliberation, he returns to his coffee. The subject is never broached in your house again.

On your errand runs into town, you start stopping to talk to Kate when you see her – the second fire spooked her pretty bad, but you do your best to take her mind off it and onto prettier ideas. You both share flights of fancy – she remarks that she's always wanted to get out of Yardley, to travel; you say you're still too young to be worrying about that, but you promise her that when the two of you are old enough, you'll take her to San Francisco. She blushes and laughs at your idea, but when you think about it, you truly hope that one day you'll be able to follow through on that promise. She sighs and comments that if not San Francisco, she'll just run away, hit the road and hop railcars like a wayfaring hobo. You make her promise to take you with her – or at least give you proper warning before she runs off.

With a few parting words and soft glances, you bid Kate goodbye and jog off to go collect your mother's groceries at the general store. On your way out, you pass Martin Way, a little ramshackle alleyway next to the general store where the gang of local hooligans gather to cook ant hills and drink cheap rye that they bribe passing townsfolk to buy for them. You normally try to avoid seeing these firebrand delinquents; they're bigger, they're older, and surely meaner than you – they're thirteen after all - but as you pass by, you see them pinning another kid to the alley wall, cackling amongst themselves.

The biggest one is a thirteen-year-old with fat cheeks and rusty colored hair named Linus, and his two twelve-year-old lackies are Ernest, a stout, cornfed little man, and Alfie, a skittish paper boy. You watch as Ernest and Alfie pin William, a quiet classmate of yours, against the wall while Linus shakes a matchbook in front of the frightened boy's nose, chanting:

"*Matchstick Man, Matchstick Man*
Lights the fire in the pan!

Matchstick Man, Matchstick Man
Not your average boogeyman!

Matchstick Man, Matchstick Man
Has a dark and fiery plan…

Matchstick Man, Matchstick Man
He'll burn you down just cause he can!"

Ernest holds William's plump fingers outstretched as Linus strikes a match, holding the dancing flame just inches away from William's quaking palm. The boy lets out yelps of pain as the match scorches a dime sized circle into his hand. That's when you feel a rock in your hand.

You pitch the stone at Linus, cracking him square in the side of the skull! The bully lets out a groan and drops the match into the dirt as a trickle of crimson blood drips from the point where the rock struck him. Linus wheels around, a burning fury in his eyes, his looming form ready to unleash every ounce of anger out on your tiny body – but before the hulking teenager can charge you, you've snatched another stone up from the dirt and are brandishing it like David ready to nail Goliath with the killing shot.

Linus doesn't dare come any closer, fearing a stone to the teeth, and without their oafish leader, Ernest and Alfie want nothing to do with the conflict at their doorstep. After a few more tense moments, Linus grumbles and scurries down the alleyway and around the corner, he and his gang shouting all sorts of nastiness over the shoulder as they flee.

As they run, you notice Kate staring at you from across the street, your silhouette framed in the mouth of the alleyway, still clutching the rock in your hand like Cain after bludgeoning his brother. Before you can say anything, much less explain yourself, she walks away down the street without a word.

You help William to his feet, your classmate still clutching his burnt hand like a war wound. He thanks you in a barely audible voice and you ask about that strange chant Linus and his boys were wailing about.

"The Matchstick Man," William explains, still composing himself. "It's some story they got told about the fires and Anabelle and Joshua dyin'. They said there's a man with straw skin and matchstick bones that came at night and burned them alive to gobble up their souls. Said he was like a scarecrow or a ghost or somethin' – and they said he was gonna get me next."

William acts like he doesn't believe in this matchstick boogieman – he's pretty smart, after all – but there's a hesitation in his voice that makes you doubt his skepticism.

"Who went and told them a silly thing like that?" you remark, trying to help calm the scattered William.

"They said Clarissa Hartman told them," William shrugs.

"Well, nobody ever knows what Clarissa is talking about," you scoff, telling William not to worry about the bully's empty threats – or, at least, that's what you hope they are.

When you return home for dinner that night, your mother mentions that she saw the Banksons on their way out of town this afternoon, with just about everything they owned strapped to their cart. Despite their struggle, the Bankson farm never recovered from the tragedy burnt into its very soil, and your father expects that they released their house to the bank to scrape together any money they could.

You immediately feel your heart sink deep into a pit in your chest, crestfallen that Kate left without saying goodbye – that her last image of you is of an angry little boy with a rock in his fist. You pipe up, asking your mother if the Bankson's daughter was with them on the cart – your mother cocks her head, but says that she didn't see any little girl with them. Hell, she didn't even know they had another child besides Joshua, but your mother shrugs and suggests that the daughter must've been sent ahead, to live with relatives until the Bankson parents found a new home. That would be the responsible thing to do.

A spark of hope ignites back inside your lonely heart – maybe Kate had finally decided to run away, like she had always said. And maybe she'd be back for you. For you and San Francisco. The little voice of reason in the rear of your skull tells you that all that is nonsense, fantasies you two had brewed up – that San Francisco couldn't really happen. That's not how these things work. But that doesn't stop you from daydreaming about a

West Coast escape with the waifish farmgirl by your side until you're snug in bed hours later.

Chink! Chink! In the middle of pale night, you awaken to a soft clacking on the glass of your bedroom window – it is the only sound that echoes through the silent October Eve.

Groggy and still in a half-dream haze, you pull yourself out of bed and over to the window – there, waiting in the moonlight-peppered grass below your bedroom is Kate, her thin form swaying in the night breeze! She beckons for you to come down, flashing you a sugar-sweet smile – you need no further convincing. You tip toe as quietly as your excited feet can carry you, down the stairs and past your parents' door. You throw on your overcoat and gingerly walk out the front door, careful to silence any rebellious creaking.

You run to embrace Kate, your soul soaring to know that she did not leave you behind. Of course not, she smiles – she had made a promise, remember? This hug is the first between you two, and though you beam over her embrace, you are careful not to squeeze too hard – up close, Kate thin body feels brittle in your arms, like she'll crack if you aren't gentle enough. You ask her why she didn't leave with her parents, but Kate just sighs and takes your hand between her chilly fingers and asks if you would walk with her for a few minutes. Of course, you assure her.

You both walk in silence for a long time, strolling across your family's farm with only the sound of the wind through the cornstalks as your companion. You notice the trees at the end of the property have begun to shed their withered leaves, covering the grassy ground with the shattered husks of the once-golden foliage. Winter's fingers are crawling across Yardley as November grows near, and you say as much to Kate, who just responds with a melancholic nod.

She doesn't say much of anything until you are nearing your front door once again – it seems she was lost in deep thought during your walk, but you don't blame her, knowing her current predicament. In your sleepy state, you don't even know how long that walk lasted, but you don't mind.

Finally, she turns to you, sadness in her expression like the day you had first seen her with your mother.

"I like you," she says, very matter of fact. This time, it is Kate that has trouble keeping her eyes off her shoes – you hope this is a good sign. "Most people don't listen when you tell them things. When you're worried, they tell you not to think about it; when you're scared, they tell you nothing can hurt you. But they don't tell you the truth."

"You tell me the truth," Kate says with a forlorn smile. "Even if the truth is just silence. It's nice to have someone to listen, listen to the silly dreams that will never happen."

"They will happen–," you begin to say, but Kate shaking head silences your protest barely after it leaves your lips.

"No, they won't," Kate frowns, letting go of your hand and turning away from you. "Not for you."

"Huh?" you ask, not sure if you heard her right. What could she mean? You run your fingers through your hair, flustered, but when you next look at your hand, you find it cold and wet, a clear viscous liquid dripping from your hair and between your fingers. Its scent is noxious, causing your nose to recoil. As you feel your own body, you realize that your whole body is drenched in the liquid. When did this happen? Why didn't you notice?

You feel a weight in your left hand, a weight that hadn't been there just seconds earlier. Looking down, you see your left fist clutching the handle of an open metal can, a trail of glistening liquid leading from the can around your homestead and off into your family's field. But that was the hand Kate had been holding – you couldn't have been carrying anything.

You raise the can high in the meager moonlight: the chipped red paint reads *lantern oil*.

You turn your confused eyes back to Kate, hoping that your friend will say something to explain away all this strangeness, but when you look at the girl, she is no longer the glassy eyed damsel you had seen on Main Street...

Kate's skin has turned a gray hue, even more ashen than her usual pallor, and golden fingers of straw jut out from beneath her frock. Her skin is lined with stitch marks and needle threads, her features haphazardly assembled into a chilling quilt of flesh and cloth. When she finally raises her face to meet your gaze, her flaxen hair parts, revealing the hidden portion of her face – beneath, her right eye is a gleaming coat button sewed into a splotch of charred burgundy fabric that makes up what remains of the right side of her face. Her remaining human eye has lost its sheen and now stares back at you, passionless and dry.

"I'm sorry," she whispers, her voice scratching out of her throat like twigs dragged against tree bark, as she takes a step towards you. You want to yell, to run back inside and pull the covers over your head until the patchwork girl disappears back into the ether from which she came, but you find your feet frozen to their place on the front stoop of your house. Your brain is screaming, but your body doesn't listen. It can't hear you. She won't let it.

Kate, if you can still call her Kate, takes your hand in hers, her fingers crunching like the sound of crushed hay with each little movement.

"You were one of the few that could see me, that could hear me," Kate says, her straw hands squeezing yours in reassurance. "But you were the only one who ever stopped to listen."

"The Banksons never had a daughter, did they?" you croak out of your fear-parched lips.

"No," Patchwork Kate admits. "But you did have a friend. That part was true."

Kate's grip relaxes as she takes a few steps backwards – try as you might, you cannot follow her. Looking down into the hand Kate had just been holding, you see a matchbox, tinged with dirt – the same matchbox you knocked from Linus' hands earlier today. You don't remember having taken it with you when you left the alley.

"Please…," you force out, the oil fumes drawing tears from your eyes, though your body remains unable to lift a hand to catch the teardrops. Your body is yours no longer.

"I'm sorry. But everyone needs to eat," Patchwork Kate says. "Even the bad things."

With a lift of her finger, you watch as your hand grips the matchbox, pulls a red-headed stick from amongst the many within, and holds it against the weathered box edge.

You strike the match. You drop it into the fuel at your feet. The flames consume you. You have no say in the matter.

It is winter in Yardley. There is smoke in the air.

SECOND SKIN

"My name is Dr. Narissa Longsteet, *and I have made a terrible mistake.*"

It was a quiet in Sedona, Arizona as the crisp desert air rolled down from the red rocks and into a tree-lined valley. At the illustrious Thurston Institute, the medical students' dreaded midterms had finally run their course, leaving the campus in a state of weary silence.

It was on an afternoon like this that a mysterious package arrived at the office door of Professor Louisa LaMorte, Deputy Director of the Institute's renown Humanities and Anthropological Sciences department. The cardboard box was bent and brutalized, its contents clearly packed in some frantic haste, the whole package held together with a manic patchwork of packing tape. There was no return label or postage on the package – there were simply three phrases, scrawled in trembling handwriting:

"To Prof. LaMorte, Thurston Institute … URGENT …" the handwriting read, each letter seemingly etched into the box with increasing tenacity. At the bottom of the box, there was a scrawled signature: "Dr. Narissa Longstreet."

Upon seeing this signature, Professor LaMorte made her way to the Institute's mailroom as quickly as her patent leather shoes could carry her, the clacking of her heels echoing through the Institute's empty white halls like footsteps reverberating through a monumental crypt. When she arrived at the mailroom, she interrogated each and every post carrier, demanding to know exactly when and how this package had arrived – and most importantly, who had delivered it.

A frenetic energy gripped Professor LaMorte's typically reserved voice as a degree of terror began to bleed out from beneath her well-polished professorial veneer. But no matter how many mailroom men she asked and no matter the vehemence in her voice, no one seemed to know where the mystery box had come from.

"Louisa," Burt, the elderly postmaster, intervened, placing a grandfatherly hand on the possessed professor's arm. "I don't know what to tell you. If none of my boys have seen it, they haven't seen it. And look – the thing don't have any postage anyhow. If this ended up at your office, that means someone came onto school grounds and hand-delivered it."

Professor LaMorte collapsed into a chair next to one of the mail bins, cradling the package in her lap while gripping her forehead between her thin fingers. Her thick rimmed glasses began to fog as tears rolled down her scarlet cheeks, her mania now replaced with a sorrowful befuddlement. Burt leaned down, offering her a kind smile to mask his own concern. You see, Louisa LaMorte was one of the powerhouses of the Thurston Institute – she had squared off against the nigh-omnipotent Dean Braxton, and even won on a few occasions. She was not a woman who was easily broken. So, to see her like this…

"What's got you so worked up, Luce?" Burt asked in a delicate voice, worried his colleague would shatter at any provocation. When Louisa LaMorte finally turned her bloodshot eyes to the postmaster, he realized that the professor's body was not quaking fingertips-to-toes out of some sadness – instead, he bore witness to pure terror, embedded deep behind her pupils.

"Narissa's been missing for five months," she explained, her voice cracked like the shards of some broken mirror. "And this is her handwriting."

As Professor LaMorte returned to her office, the box seemed to grow heavier her hands with each step down the hall. Narissa had been her colleague, her friend. They had both attended Princeton for their graduate studies – Narissa earning her doctorate in Anthropology with a focus on Pre-Colonial American Civilizations while Louisa earned her master's in Archeology and Linguistics. Afterwards, they both decided to apply for research grants at the distinguished Thurston Institute, promising to have each other's backs in the cutthroat world of academia.

As Louisa steadily climbed the ladder into the higher echelons of the Institute's administration, Narissa remained at the bottom of the proverbial totem pole, content to continue her days as a field researcher. Narissa had always been most comfortable in the dirt with her subjects – objectivity was not something that often bothered Narissa in her pursuit of knowledge. Perhaps that 'truth above all' attitude was what put her at odds with so many other members of the Thurston faculty, Dean Braxton in particular.

Even as Louisa became increasingly enveloped in the folds of institutional academia, she did her best to defend her friend when the tenure board came skulking about or the grant committees questioned the necessity of Narissa's research. But no matter how Louisa would smooth things over or whatever departmental sway she was able to lend her Longstreet, Narissa's mouth always found a way to get her into worse trouble.

It wasn't that what Narissa said was wrong – often quite the opposite, as she lambasted the Institute's exclusionary policies and its faculty full of lazy intellectuals-turned—armchair-professors placated by years of tenured complacency – but Narissa lacked the backhanded diplomacy that was required to climb the rungs of the academic world. Louisa was sometimes ashamed of how well she inhabited that role herself.

When tensions finally came to a head and Louisa could no longer smother the fire of contempt that was blazing through the faculty ready to consume Narissa, she came up with the only solution that she could: she sent Narissa away on a research sabbatical. She didn't care what subject Narissa studied or where she wanted to go – she just knew that she had to put some distance between Narissa and the Thurston higher-ups before they finally snapped and killed her scientific career for good. The Institute has a lot of sway in the realms of both science and politics, making them a very dangerous enemy should they deem you a threat to their establishment comforts.

Narissa either couldn't see that or didn't care, so Louisa made the choice for her.

That was six months ago. Narissa had decided to travel to the Navajo Nation in the northern high desert of Arizona for her studies. She had always had a good relationship with the Southwestern tribes, having written a number of beautiful papers on their plights to rebuild their slowly-eroding culture. Narissa saw herself as a witness, meant to observe the twilight era of these proud peoples and, if nothing more, preserve their legacy in the annals of anthropological history.

For the first few weeks, Narissa sent reports back detailing her progress. They weren't thrilling updates by any means – scheduling interviews, coordinating lodging, the like – and they certainly didn't give Louisa the sense that anything was wrong. But only a month after her sabbatical began, Narissa's updates stopped. She didn't answer her phone, she didn't send any progress memos, and her grant money dried up.

The Institute wanted to write Dr. Longsteet off as a failure, a thief, or both, and in turn validate every poisonous thing they had ever said about her. But Louisa couldn't believe Narissa would've quit or run off, not without leaving some sign to let her know she was okay. They were friends, weren't they?

As the weeks ticked by, Louisa became increasingly worried with each silent day that passed. Eventually, she called the Navajo Police up in Window Rock and had them perform a wellness check – but when they checked the villages that Narissa had described visiting in her early reports, not only did they find no signs of the missing anthropologist, but the villagers all claimed they had no idea who Narissa Longstreet even was. It was like Narissa had ceased to exist. She begged the police to put out an APB on Narissa, to find her before she got herself into more trouble, but the Navajo Police were already short on resources to begin with. With no evidence of foul play, there wasn't much they could do.

"I guess that's the beauty of America, Professor," a police lieutenant with a sunbaked baritone voice had said to her over a crackling phone line. "In this country, it's still legal to disappear if you want to."

As weeks turned to months with no word of Narissa's whereabouts, Louisa began to be plagued by doubts about her friend. Had she really just run off with the grant money? Had this all been one final act of defiance against Braxton and his ivory tower ilk? Did Narissa think Louisa had abandoned her? Had they actually been the friends that Louisa thought they were?

But no matter how many questions she asked, no answers ever appeared – disappointing, especially to a scientist. But this wasn't something that Louisa could research and dissect and write some dissertation on – matters of the human heart had always been more Narissa's forte. She was ashamed to admit it, but eventually even Louisa gave up on her search for the missing Dr. Longstreet, instead choosing to return to her safety bubble of academic ambivalence.

Until this afternoon, that is. Until the package arrived.

Louisa finally made it back to her office, locking the door to prevent any unwarranted intrusions before sweeping the dusty textbooks and half-graded essays off her desk to make way for whatever lurked beneath the box's cardboard shell.

With a glinting pen knife shaped like an ornate peacock – a gift from Narissa from a few birthdays back – Professor LaMorte delicately sliced open the taped edges of the package. As Louisa gently bent back the box flaps, a dollop of what appeared to be pale, vicious slime dripped down from one of the errant lengths of tape onto her desk, bringing with it a putrid, sour smell that threatened to make the Professor gag with only the slightest whiff. Unable to stand the stench, Louisa quickly wiped the glob away with a tissue and tossed it into her trash can, though the substance left behind a shimmering, oily sheen on her pinewood desk.

Emptying out the box with an extra dose of caution, Louisa found it filled with manilla folders, stuffed with files and research dating back to the beginning of the sabbatical. It was Narissa's field notes! But as Professor LaMorte combed through the papers, she found that with each passing month, Narissa's reports became increasingly sloppy and disorganized, dotted with stapled notes and nonsense drawings, until the final few documents – dated as recently as last month – were written on crumpled scraps of notebook paper in the same frantic penmanship that was carved into the box's exterior. However, the most important discovery was still to come.

Unsure if she was being propelled by mounting fear or a creeping curiosity, Louisa dared to dig deeper into the box and soon produced a smaller, plastic container, filled with a collection of sand-dusted cassette tapes. Running to her closet, Louisa dug out an old cassette player from the recesses of the clutter left behind by professors past. Narissa had found the old relic when she helped move Louisa into her office all those years ago – and Dr. Longstreet knew Professor LaMorte well enough to know that she never threw things away, especially weird old junk. It was the anthropologists in them both, they had always joked.

The cassette player was in bad shape, its chrome plating dented, and its lettering scratched away by the relentless march of time – but when Louisa pressed down on the weathered red button at the base of the device, its cassette deck popped open with an analog *ca-chunk*, beckoning the professor to slip a tape into its dark mechanical innards. Whether she was motivated by her thirst for knowledge or a genuine desire to help her colleague, it didn't really matter – Professor Louisa LaMorte picked up the cassette tape marked *"Play First"*, spun the cassette gears back, and hit play.

At first, there was only crackling silence, the soundwaves occasionally warped by the aged cassette player's mechanisms... until a voice finally pierced the white noise:

"My name is Dr. Narissa Longstreet and I've made a terrible mistake," the voice spoke through the static of the tape gears. *"This package, and the tapes and field notes within, are meant for Professor Louisa LaMorte, Deputy Director of Humanities and Anthropological Sciences at the Thurston Institute – Her and her alone."*

Salt tears began to brim at the corner of Louisa's eyes as she heard the voice of her long-lost friend for the first time in six months. It wasn't until she heard Narissa say her name again that Louisa realized just how much she had truly missed her.

However, as Professor LaMorte composed herself, she began to realize that there was something off about her colleague's voice. Something vacant, something haunting. Narissa's words seemed to slur and ebb, as if she was trying to speak while struggling to keep her head from submerging beneath some dark, unseen waters.

"If this package has somehow ended up in the wrong hands, I beg you, whoever you are, to stop listening right now, burn everything, and forget you ever found this box," Narissa continued, her voice cold and commanding. After a brief pause punctuated by a chest-rattling cough, Dr. Longstreet spoke again, this time with a measure of compassion in her weary words. *"Now that that's over and done with, I hope that I'm addressing Louisa directly. Hi Luce."*

"Hi..." Louisa murmured without thinking, the fragile greeting escaping from her lips.

"I'm sure that you have a lot of questions. I'm sorry I won't be able to answer them in person," Narissa continued before being interrupted by a

sharp, pained breath, as if she had just been stabbed in the side by some invisible dagger. *"But that's what this box is for. I've collected all my notes and audio logs from the very start of this nightmare. I wish I knew when exactly this all went wrong but… it's… it's been getting harder to think clearly the last few weeks."*

"I can't piece it together anymore… I'm too far gone," Narissa slurred, her energy waning with each word, each passing syllable painful for her to pronounce. Louisa wanted to reach for her, yank Narissa herself out of the tape and hold her close! But even now, she remembered that what she heard, the echoes of Narissa's pained words, were just hollow facsimiles of the real woman. The real Narissa was still somewhere out there, missing.

"But you… you'll know what to do. Go back through my tapes, figure out what happened, and do what needs to be done. You'll… ack!... know when the time comes. You'll know, you'll kNAAAAGGGHHHH!"

The end of the recording erupted with a dissonant, bloodcurdling scream that filled the room with such ambient horror that Louisa had to slam the eject button before the malicious sound could burrow its way any deeper into her skull! The cassette player coughed out the tape – even the machine was glad to be rid of whatever shadows lurked in those sound waves. Had that been Narissa screaming? It barely sounded human. Or, more accurately, it had sounded like the voices of many humans, all wailing and shrieking at once to create a terrible chorus of sickening harmonies. It must have been a damaged tape, Louisa tried to convince herself.

Louisa didn't dare rewind the tape to listen again, so she instead turned her attention to the other cassettes in the box – Narissa's audio logs. Steeling her nerves in preparation for whatever madness might be seared into those vinyl strips, Louisa listened to each, doing her best to transcribe the information found within, hoping that doing so would reveal some path to her friend's salvation. How wrong she was.

Audio Log #1 - March 5th

"Hello, hello! Test 1-2-3. They better not have scammed me on this thing…"

"Alright, well this is audio log number one, Dr. Narissa Longstreet report-ing to you live from the middle of sand-blasted Arizona! But seriously, as far as updates go, I've set up shop in a rented RV in some little town called Bitter Canyon, right on the edge of the Navajo Nation – thus begins my research sabbatical, bankrolled by the Thurston Institute. I purchased this recorder from some second-hand shop in Flagstaff, since everyone knows I work better when I speak my thoughts aloud – though some people would argue that's why I got sent out here in the first place. But discoveries don't get made until someone has the guts to push the envelope, right? At least that's how I see it."

"The purpose of this sabbatical is to research the medicinal and spiritual practices of the Navajo shamans, a subject the anthropological world has had little success in studying to any real degree. That's by design. The Navajo are incredibly guarded with the secrets and cultural practices of their people, and for good reason. Now, they don't mind sharing the feathers and the rain dancing – sure, they respect those traditions, but that's surface level stuff to appease the tourists bused in on day trips from the Grand Canyon. The real esoteric knowledge has been kept away from the eyes of academia and the outside world – until now, or at least so I hope."

"I've made contact with a few of my sources within the Navajo Nation to try to schedule meetings with some village elders and medicine men, but I don't want to speak to the same shamans that are on the talking head rosters of every Nat Geo show. I'm trying to dig deeper, find some sources that are hidden from public view. I know if Louisa – I mean, Professor LaMorte – was here, she would scold me about keeping my objectivity, but I think there's merit to getting in the mud and showing your subjects that you're worthy of the knowledge you're seeking. I intend to prove my mettle, to the Navajo, to the Institute…"

"But first, dinner – which tonight is Hormel chili con tin can on this RV's range stove. Let's hope I don't blow up this rust bucket on Night One. What a waste of Institute resources that would be."

Audio Log #2 – April 2nd

"I'm not ashamed to admit it – I'm getting pretty frustrated around here. It's been nearly a month and the Navajo have been stonewalling me at every turn. I've only been able to schedule a handful of interviews with old maids and local priests, and all I'm getting from them are recipes for aloe salves and children's stories – all things the Smithsonian has heard about a hundred times over. And it's not just some 'stranger danger' mentality – I've interviewed some of these sources before on other projects, but now they're keeping me at an arm's length."

"There's this old theory about the native people being more attuned to reading the auras of those around them, and I'm starting to believe it. Everyone in these villages I visit keeps looking at me with these dark eyes, distrusting me before I even get a word in. It's like they know what I'm here for… and at this point I wish they'd tell me what that is, cause damned if I know."

"I do have one lead I got from some farm kid – he was saying that there's a man named Tokala living on a homestead near Spider Rock that might be able to help me. Kid didn't say much and he kept looking over his shoulder as he talked, but the boy said that Tokala had once been a shaman but defected to go live a solitary life after something happened to his brother. The kid said it had to do something with 'yi noldoshi', whatever that means. Didn't give me much to go on, but I'm going to make a few calls and see what I can come up with."

Audio Log #3 – April 3rd

"Alright! It is now… 8:10am on April 3rd. I stayed up all night working and I have some incredible developments to record from the last twenty-four hours, but my eyes are way too tired to write any of it down. Anyway, here goes.

First off, I made some calls to see if I could find out more about this Tokala character and thankfully the boys over at Navajo PD didn't disappoint. It took a bit of palm greasing to get me the info I needed, but I'm sure the Institute will overlook a few hundred dollars in 'consulting fees'. They over-look plenty worse all the time... but back to Tokala."

"The farm boy was right with most of his details, vague as they were – his full name is Tokala Fineday and he was a local healer up until a few years ago. That is, until his younger brother, Chayton Fineday, got caught up in what seems like a pretty grizzly double murder. Even with the bribe, the Navajo police were pretty hesitant to talk about the incident, but I think I was able to coax the general story out of them. Apparently, Chayton was seen fleeing his village after leaving a friend's home absolutely drenched in blood while two others – the homeowner and his wife – were found brutalized inside.

"The cops wouldn't go into much detail, but we're talking about 'limbs torn off' eviscerated here. That's the reason that most of the police think that it was some drug-related killing, seeing as the Native population has been battling a pretty severe opioid epidemic for the last thirty years. It must have been PCP or meth or whatever that stuff was that had some guy eating another man's face down in Florida a few years back – what else could've given Chayton the strength to do that to two people?"

"Either way, Chayton took off into the desert before the police could get there, so Tokala gave chase. No one really knows what happened out in the bush that night – all they're sure about is that when morning came,

Chayton was dead and Tokala was never the same. Official report says that Tokala killed Chayton with a gunshot to the head, but my source on the force says that wasn't really what happened – Tokala didn't even own a gun! He said that Chayton's body was pretty mangled when Tokala led them back to it, but everyone took pity on the brother for 'doing what needed to be done', so they wrote a kinder death into the official report."

"Tokala was set free after the cops accepted his self-defense plea – though chasing your brother into the desert to bash his head in hardly sounds like self-defense to me – but either way, he left his post at the village the next day, bought a spot of land up near Spider Rock, and has been living in self-imposed solitude ever since. They say he's not someone I should be afraid of, that he's a gentle man that got dealt a bad hand, but even my source admitted he wasn't sure who Tokala really was deep down inside. Not after that night."

"Oh! Oh! With all that true crime narration I almost forgot the other thing I found! I called up an old friend from the Princeton linguistics department, Dr. Rich Zorell – he and Louisa dated way back when. Anyway, I called in a favor and asked him about the phrase the farm kid said – you should have seen how white his face turned when I told him, and I don't think it was my horrific pronunciation that spooked him. Turns out the kid had actually been saying 'yee naaldlooshii', which translates from Navajo to English as 'with it, he goes on all fours'– better known as SKINWALKER!"

"For anyone unaware, a skinwalker is a creature from Native myth. There are a dozen different versions of the legend depending on which tribes you ask, but they're most commonly known as shamans or healers that were turned towards evil powers – often through rituals of human sacrifice or cannibalism – and in turn were granted the ability to shapeshift into any animal or person they so desired. There's a whole laundry list of other powers they were thought to have, from mind control to spells that destroy crops, but those are all open to debate depending on your source. The only *elements truly agreed upon are that they are shapeshifters, they are dark magicians with evil intent, and there is always a blood price to be paid for using their cursed magic."*

"There's next to no real anthropological data on the skinwalker phenomenon because it is one of the secrets that the Navajo outright refuse to discuss with outsiders — most of what is known about them comes from word-of-mouth legends or pure fiction. If Chayton was — or believed himself to be — a skinwalker, Tokala could be an incredible lens into understanding this magic or psychosis or whatever it might be. And a discovery like that... well, it would be nice to see my name in print again after so much time."

"I had an intermediary help me set up a meeting with this reclusive healer and, shockingly enough, Tokala agreed to see me. It's a three hour drive across the Navajo lands to Spider Rock, so I'm going to prep an overnight bag, try to force myself to sleep, and start making my way towards Fineday's place in a couple hours. I'm aiming to arrive before dark, but if not, a full moon is always good for a scary story."

Audio Log #3 – April 4th

"It is... 12:10am on April 4th, and I can't sleep. Just can't. Not after tonight. So I decided that you, me, and Jim Beam could have a conversation. Maybe all this will make sense if I just... talk it out, yknow? I guess I should start back at the beginning. But that means pouring another round."

"So, I took the trip out to Spider Rock to see Tokala. He lives in this, like, hippie sort of place. An airstream with some clothes lines and some lawn furniture, with some little herb garden or something off to the side. And shamans drive Chevys, if you were wondering.

Anyway, I pull in and he's sitting out on a folding chair beneath the glow of this buzzing fly zapper — who knows how long he had been sitting out there, watching, like a gargoyle with Parliament cigarettes. I asked to bum a cig off him, and that seemed to take him by surprise at first. He asked if I was the scientist, I said yes. Then all nine mother-loving feet of Tokala stood up, the big man stomped out his cigarette and said, 'We'd better talk inside.' I didn't get my smoke, but whatever – I was in. I saw him throw a glance over his shoulder before he closed the airstream door."

"The inside of the airstream was pretty sparse – looks pretty similar to my Winnebago honestly, though he lined his place with shag carpeting and all these colorful mismatched lamps so at least his tin can had some personality. But honestly, it was a nice enough place, whatever. He sat me down and offered me whiskey – some local brand I'd never heard of – and of course, I agreed. I drank moreso to earn his trust and to show my appreciation, but he was drinking for some other reason. Something real dark behind his eyes gave it away as they darted to the corners of the room every couple seconds. Then it hit me. All the lamps in his trailer weren't decor – Tokala was afraid of the dark, or what might be hiding in it."

"Now, Tokala had agreed to talk to me on two conditions: that he was to remain anonymous in my dissertation and that I couldn't record the conversation, with a notepad or a recorder. I tried to convince him otherwise, but he said that what he was about to tell me was too dangerous to be put on any kind of record – I could only walk away with what I could remember, and if I could corroborate those findings with outside evidence, then so be it."

"I… I'm sort of not proud of it, but I did try to record Tokala without him knowing, using one of those digital pocket recorders you can get at Brookstone. But when I checked it after I left, the whole recorder was all shorted out! It was brand new! Must've sat on it or something…"

"After some pleasantries neither of us really meant, we got to talking. It took some prodding, but after assuring him that I wasn't some Weekly World News reporter and that I was here to research the truth about his experience, Mr. Fineday finally told me what happened. He said that he and his brother, Chayton, were both healers, like their grandfather before *them. However, something started to get a hold of Chayton… what did he call it?… oh yeah, a 'malicious haze'. This was after Chayton was beaten during a pipeline protest in Utah."*

"Heavily concussed, it took him a long while to recover, and when he was back on his feet, Chayton's personality seemed to have totally changed. He was lethargic but violent, confused but volatile. To my limited knowledge, it sounded like frontal lobe damage, but Tokala said that some around their town began to see it as an omen that Chayton had been possessed by some evil entity."

"His radicalized rhetoric since the pipeline beating hadn't helped his image either — he would be seen walking the village roads, yelling to himself and any man, woman, or saguaro that would listen about the tyranny of the United States and their 'little green hit men', which is what he called the National Guardsmen that had tried to stove his face in. Though Tokala didn't disagree with Chayton's frustrations, his brother was starting to frighten their neighbors by talking about the coming of 'a war beneath' and 'a Great Death' that he would usher in to finally free their people. Tokala did his best to keep Chayton inside when his fits would become particularly violent."

"After Chayton was seen running through the town at night, half clothed and frenzied, some villagers wanted Chayton examined by the elders, others wanted him arrested, and there were even those who whispered about exile. Make the madman the desert's problem — I'm pretty familiar with that sort of treatment, aren't I, Louisa?"

"But enough about me. Tokala, he said that he hated telling this part of the story most of all, because it was the moment when he stopped recognizing his brother. He was planning to take Chayton out to Arizona State Psychiatric Hospital, but one morning, he woke up to find Chayton's window smashed and his brother gone. No one saw him for days — and to most of the village, that was fine by them. Like a wounded dog, Chayton had slunk off to some

rocky hideaway to die. That is, until he showed up at Atsa Bylilly's doorstep three weeks later, skeletal and possessed by some wildness. Atsa and his wife Odina had been longtime friends of the Fineday brothers – they grew up together, drank and watched football on Atsa's rabbit ear television – so they didn't have a second thought about inviting Chayton inside."

"Now, this part gets hazy, since the only witnesses to the event are either Chayton or have been vivisected, but Tokala did his best to piece events together from what he knows. As Atsa brought the malnourished Chayton over to their couch to lay him down, Odena went for the phone to ring Tokala to give him the news. When I asked Tokala why she didn't call the cops first, he just shrugged and said, 'There's 130 police officers to cover all 27,000 miles of the Navajo Nation – I was the faster option.'"

"But Odena was only thirty seconds into the call with Tokala when he heard these awful cracking sounds and screams from the other end of the line. Odena started sobbing, calling Atsa's name until her voice broke. She must have left the phone dangling off its receiver because Tokala heard her go for the front door and fumble with the lock before there was another scream and a loud, wet thud! After that, all he could hear was the buzzing of the phone line's electricity and some soggy, churning sound. 'Like masticating,' Tokala had described it. 'Like someone chewing a mouthful of thick paste right next to the receiver.'"

"Like the good brother he is – or was, I guess – Tokala ran over to the Bylilly's house, just in time to watch Chayton sprint off into the desert, covered in their friends' blood. I wish he had more details about Atsa and Odena, but Tokala got real quiet and said he didn't dare go inside – I guess the context clues were enough for him to realize there wasn't anyone in there left to save."

"Adrenalin kicked in and the big man followed his brother's blood trail out onto the mesa – that is, until he ran headlong into a massive wolf! This beast was huge, its fur mangey and matted with blood, its rumbling growl roiling through a body nearly the size of an adult bear. Tokala assured me that they didn't have animals larger than coyotes out in these parts. It was during the moonlight standoff that Tokala clocked that the wolf's eyes were distinctly human — a classic skinwalker trait from the old myths."

"Realizing that this was indeed his brother, Tokala put his hands in the air and begged Chayton to wait, to talk to him. The wolf just… stopped, its disfigured face frozen in this look of surprise. And then… well, this part gets a little hard to believe, but if you can stand to swallow your Master's Degree for a second and suspend your disbelief, you might just realize that this could be the biggest discovery to hit mainstream science in decades."

"The way Tokala tells it… the wolf — Chayton — started to shudder and shake, like the dog was having some kind of seizure. But as the shaking got more and more violent, the wolf's spine began to buckle and crack until it split its own skin, leaving shreds of flesh and fur slopping off its haunches like melting wax left out in the sun. Shedding its skin like a cicada, the wolf — if you could still call the amalgamation of disjointed limbs and sinew a 'wolf' — seemed to break its ankles, then its knees, as it stood up on its back legs and wailed in a 'legion of moans', as Tokala described it. Its skull shifted beneath the thin coating of muscle and membrane that was still stretched over the creature's bones, Tokala watching its snout crunch back into itself until the face became this twisted, half-melted human scream. The only thing that never changed was the poor monster's eyes. That scream swirled again and after a new layer of skin had stitched itself into place… there was Chayton, standing in the moonlight, naked, bloody, and smiling."

"Chayton started rambling to Tokala, about how he was glad that his brother was there, that they could be the start of some new day for the Navajo, but Tokala didn't have a damn clue what he was talking about. When Chayton finally uttered the word 'skinwalker', his eyes lit up with this manic enthusiasm — yes, he had gone back in the old knowledge, scoured the desert for all the right ingredients, and he had done it! He had recreated *the potion that the shamans had once used to transform themselves into these beings of flesh and unlimited potential."*

"Chayton knew that these practices had been deemed dark magic, but he didn't give a shit. He knew that, to beat back the American oppressors, he would need to use everything at their peoples' disposal – even become a killer. Atsa and Odena's blood had been the final component to the ritual. The old legends say that to become One with the Flesh, you must spill the blood of a loved one for the transformation to be complete. Not sure if that had any effect on the physiological changes bestowed by this potion, but the psychological aftermath was clear."

"Do I agree with his methods…. Who's to say? But do I respect his loyalty to his people, as twisted as his interpretation might've been? Hell yes. A few folks at the Institute could stand to learn that lesson… or be on the receiving end of it."

"But Tokala didn't see things that way. He stood there on that mesa, listening to his brother's ramblings, knowing that it was his job as a healer to put an end to this madness. He could see that Chayton was exhausted from his transformation and knew that if he didn't take his shot then… well, there might not be a next time. So, he opened those big arms of his and asked his brother to come to him. Chayton, thinking that Tokala was going to go along with the plan, embraced his brother. He held Chayton close and he… he whispered… God, I'm too drunk to be telling this… he said 'You're my brother, I'll always love you.' And then he put a buck knife through Chayton's chest."

"Immediately, Chayton's body began to morph and transform as the skin-walker side of him fought back, almost instinctively like some cornered animal. His head split apart and his thrashing body began to sprout more limbs, flailing to fight back, but Tokala didn't let up. You see, when Chayton had changed from his wolf form, Tokala had watched closely, and between all the melting skin and twisting bone, he saw one thing that never changed,

buried beneath the rest of Chayton's mailable flesh – his brother's heart. The one organ a skinwalker can't replace.

"So Tokala drove the blade deeper and deeper, even as he felt Chayton's liquid flesh beginning to burn against his own skin. It wasn't until Tokala felt the blade force its way through his diaphragm and pierce Chayton's still-beating heart that the big man let go, watching his brother stumble backwards and collapse into a writhing mound of fingers and faces and pain. As the life faded from the skinwalker, Chayton became nothing more than a twisted puddle of parts, his eyes the last things to melt away. Even then, Tokala said he could see the betrayal and the... loneliness in his brother's gaze. That's how the cops found him."

"Sure, it was a good story, but I didn't believe it until Tokala showed me his arm. He kept his sleeves rolled down even though it was a toasty night, but when he rolled them up, he revealed these insane scars lining his forearm where Chayton's flesh had tried bonding with his. They weren't burn scars or cuts or something simple like that – they were these pock marks, hundreds of little holes burrowed into his skin, like you'd see in coral or on some sea sponge. Chayton had literally tried to siphon the meat off his brother's bones. Imagine the trust issues this guy must be dealing with these days."

"He said that when he returned home after answering the cops' questions, he found something left on his back stoop – something from Chayton. There was a note, full of the same sorts of ramblings he had already heard from his brother on the mesa, tied to the neck of a mason jar full of this purple, viscous liquid. Chayton had been serious about his older brother joining him – he had made a second batch of the skinwalker potion in the hopes that Tokala would take the dive. That's when things started to get tense... I asked him if he still had it."

"The big guy got real quiet for a second, but I didn't dare ask again. Eventually, he admitted that he had held on to the potion but had never considered drinking it or even opening the lid. 'As long as it's with me, its evil isn't *off somewhere in the wrong hands' is how he justified it. But who is this washed-up hermit to decide whose hands are the right ones?"*

"I mean, think about it! Forget all the magic horseshit! If this formula can do what Tokala says it can — and we've got the scars and corpses to prove it can — breaking down the science behind it could be lifesaving! World changing! We're talking about the conscious manipulation of the body down to a cellular level — that means no more tumors, no more birth defects, no more gender dysmorphia. Hell, we're talking about making the very act of surgery obsolete! There is unlimited potential hidden in these ancient traditions that's ours to harness now that we have the capacity to understand them on a scientific level!"

"But that's not how Tokala saw things. He refused to look at the bigger picture. After he realized that I wouldn't back down, his face turned real cold, real serious, and he said it was time for me to leave. I drove across half of Arizona to see this guy and he kicked me out after forty-five minutes! Whatever, I'm used to suffering at the hand of little, nearsighted people..."

"No, you know what? Screw this! I'm going back. Tonight. I'll make him understand how important this is! He has to..."

"Think this bottle can last me all the way back to Spider Rock?"

Audio Log #4 – April 4th (cont.)

(Note: Blood found smeared on edge of cassette tape, dried.)

"Things didn't go to plan. Tokala is dead. But I found it."

"I got back here, to Tokala's airstream, by 3:30 - 4 a.m. I expected him to be asleep, maybe drunk like me. I had something prepared to say that I had rehearsed on the drive over, but I was just as ready to sneak in and try to find the jar myself if he was knocked out. It would've been simpler that way. But as I pulled up, with my headlights off... there he was. Sitting

out under that fly zapper, waiting for me with a shotgun in his hand. I guess Tokala had finally bought a gun since the last time Navajo PD had checked in on him."

"I tried to keep cool, but my head was swimming from the booze and the hum of the fluorescent mosquito light… I got out of my car, hands in the air, asked him what this was all about. He said he knew that I would be back to take the potion from him — he had seen it in my eyes. 'A masochistic greed', he said. Same as he saw in Chayton. I took a few steps forward and I asked him to hear me out, but he wasn't having it. He raised that shotgun and pointed it right at my chest, so close the barrel nearly pressed up against my forehead."

"But I saw something in his eyes — I saw fear. Not fear of what I would do to him, but fear of what he was considering doing to me. And that made him weak, just for a second. I grabbed the shotgun barrel and tried to point it away from my head, but he panicked and pulled the trigger! A second too late to blow a hole in my chest but just in time to blast my right ear to pieces with buckshot!"

"It was all high-pitched ringing and warm blood pouring down my chin… I wobbled, my balance was shot, and Tokala looked like he was about to be sick. He had turned the side of my head into pulled pork and he didn't have the guts to finish the job. Knowing that I only had a few precious moments before blood loss took me, I scrambled for the shotgun! We wrestled over the hunk of metal — Tokala begged me to let go, but I was fighting for my life. Something took over and before I knew it, the gun ended up going off, pressed right up beneath the big man's chin. In the blink of an eye, Tokala Fineday's head was nothing more special than a burst melon scattered across some lonely highway shoulder. But I wasn't one to talk — my skull was a leaking boat, held together with scraps and losing blood by the second."

"I was going to pass out or just plain bleed out in front of that airstream if I didn't think of something quickly. Only one thing came to mind: finish the

mission. I stumbled through the trailer door and just started tearing that place to pieces. Cabinets, coffee cans, clothing drawers – I ripped them all apart looking for that jar, but I found nothing. He had hidden it well and I was running out of time as my blood pressure continued to drop."

"But funnily enough, that's what did it – when I collapsed in the airstream, I felt this bump under the shag carpeting! In a last ditch effort, I just dug into the rug with my nails like a wild animal and tore it off its pinnings, revealing a loose floorboard underneath! I picked up the board as delicately as my quaking hand could lift it and there it was – the potion, tucked away in a dusty little crawl space where Tokala hoped no one would ever find it. At first, it looked like some inconspicuous portion of leftovers sealed away in its scratched up, painfully ordinary mason jar. Funny how such a simple thing had already cost four people their lives."

"By that point my vision had started to blur and this numbing shock was creeping up from the tips of my limbs – I was fading. Didn't have time to think… I drank it, Luce."

"For a second, nothing happened. The potion was thick and rancid like bile – I was worried I was about to throw it up, like the time when I did peyote back in college. But I forced the mouthful down and after a few seconds, I felt a cramping in my guts and this swelling in my throat and then – fire. Fire in my blood. Pumping through every inch of me as my whole body contorted on that airstream floor, against my will like I was hooked up to some electroshock machine. I wish I could describe it better… maybe when my head clears… but as my body broke and rebuilt itself, my brain was just bombarded with these spectral colors and knowledge I can't put into human words no matter how hard I try. I could feel every tendon, every length of nerve and sinew in me like some great organic motherboard.

"I watched as the side of my face boiled and bubbled before these strands of skin began to stitch me back together like some flesh quilt… but after a few seconds, my ear was back and the scars were gone. I looked in a nearby

mirror and saw that I was perfectly unharmed... even improved! All my blemishes, my scarred-over wounds and cigarette burns from the bad old days were gone, like the Flesh knew what I wanted without me even having to ask! The only thing that spooked me for a second was when I noticed one of my eyes now had two different pupils, each looking off in a different direction with minds of their own — but with a moment of concentration, I brought them back together. Mental cellular control after just seconds."

"Now I'm sitting in my car, recording this message. I have to keep a record of the process if we even hope to understand how this works. I feel electri-fied... like I'm having seven thoughts at once... and I can understand all of them! I still have this sick pit in the base of my stomach every time I look out the windshield and see Tokala lying there, all... you know. But he pulled the gun on me! And at least his death means something, right? He's gifted humanity with its next Great Leap Forward — he just had to give his life to do it. I'll make sure he's remembered as a hero."

"I should.... I should hit the road before the sun comes up. I don't know how many visitors Tokala gets out here, but I shouldn't stick around to find out. A few Navajo PD guys know I came to see him, but with the bribes in their pockets, who knows if they'll talk. They'll stall, it'll buy me some time... and besides, now I have the best disguise in the world."

Audio Log #5 - June (Date Unknown)

"Narissa Longstreet here in... well, I guess it's better if I don't say what city. Don't want to leave any breadcrumbs. It's been a while since my last recording, I just... I've been getting carried away with my new life as a skinwalker. It's like being a god — one of the trickster kind — and goddamn it's fun. I've been training my body to control my new abilities. It was a slow process but now... now I'm a natural. I'll break it down for research's sake."

"At first, every transformation was painful, even the little ones. I started with something simple – changing my eye color – and I practiced for days in motel bathrooms, just staring in the mirror till my baby blues turned brown… then purple... then black. Then I started to change the rest of me – my hair and my face all came pretty naturally but changing things like my height and weight… those really hurt. Those ones require you to either disintegrate parts of your bones or stitch new parts together, and neither process is fun. I also realized early on that you can only transform organic parts of yourself – that means no shapeshifting your clothes, and if you turn yourself into an animal, you'd better stay that way until you get back to your safehouse or else you'll be walking the streets stark naked."

"When I first began training, I could only transform maybe once a day, and holding that form took an immense amount of concentration that left me exhausted. But after a month or two, I've been able to harness my powers and now I'm shapeshifting on a whim, sometimes just for the hell of it. I know you wouldn't approve, Luce, but I had to push the limits of the skin-walker form, put it through a pressure test. Scientific method and all that."

"I started by impersonating people I'd see on the street – I'd watch from a park bench and see how well I could replicate a passerby's features after only a few seconds of exposure. Sometimes they would turn out like half-finished Play-doh sculptures, but eventually I got pretty good at it. Sometimes I would keep the transformation going even when they turned and saw me – the look on these peoples' faces when they would lock eyes with themselves? Priceless!"

"Soon I was using it for all kinds of mischief – impersonating businessmen so I could drive away from hotel valets in their fancy cars, copying a club owner's face to get service in some exclusive bar downtown, shapeshifting into some lady's shitty husband and starting a scene in a restaurant just because I could. With my sabbatical money all dried up, I've been casing banks to keep myself afloat. I'll go inside and act like I'm opening *an account, but I'm really looking for one thing — the branch manager's photo hanging behind the bank teller counter. I'll come back the next day, wearing the same suit and the same face as the bank manager, acting like I'm performing some 'last minute money transfer' for the bank's corporate overlords and BAM! I'm walking out of there with a briefcase full of money and the tellers are none the wiser. Sure, maybe those bank managers took the fall a day or two later, but by then I'd already be half a state away. And what sociopath has any sympathy for bankers anyway?"*

"I'm sure that might rub some of you the wrong way — some of you people that are content to follow the rules that keep you nailed like a butterfly to a cork board — but you know what? It felt good to be bad. To take what was owed to me after everything else I've had to deal with in my miserable little life. And let me tell you — when I'm walking around as a man, I get everything I want. No one questions me, no one asks where I'm going, no one tells me what I should and shouldn't do. Now I see where men like Dean Braxton get their sheer audacity: from a world that coddles and waits on them just because of what they have between their legs.

"Doesn't change the fact that they're still pigs... but now the swine don't know when the wolf is lurking among them, wearing the skin of their brother to trick them into opening their pen to me. And I like the hunt."

Audio Log #6 – Unmarked Tape (Believed to be July)

(Research Note: Narissa's voice sounds duplicated or reverberated in this recording.)

"This one's all for you, Luce, wherever you are. I bet you'll never get this message, but you never listened to what I had to say before so why start now? No, you just swept me off to some middle of nowhere, do-nothing assignment so I wouldn't keep casting a shadow on your Institute aspirations. And don't act like sending those cops to come find me was some act

of kindness. Thankfully, they didn't have a clue where I'd gone – too little too late, Lucey. Lately, I've been feeling this darkness growing in me, this... anger that I never let myself feel before. Because God forbid a woman show a little goddamn frustration!"

"But you know what, Luce? Even after all the daggers you put in my back, I'm still looking out for you – like always. I'm sure you're really enjoying your new position as deputy director, aren't you? But do you know how someone becomes a deputy director? The old director has to suddenly 'step away', leaving the faculty in a convenient lurch for you to weasel your way in to fill the void. Isn't that what Professor Schofield did a few weeks back, Luce?"

"And it wasn't his rampant narcissism or the unwanted advances towards his female grad students that finally got the lecherous old fool ejected from the Institute's good graces – no, he retired with full honors and pension to go 'spend time with his grandkids.' Or at least, that's what you all believed."

"Schofield doesn't have grandkids, but no one bothered to check. Hell, when you shook Professor Schofield's hand on the day of his sudden retirement, did you happen to notice anything... off about him, Luce? A slight twinkle in his eye? A cruel curl at the edge of his grin? That's because you weren't shaking hands with Leonard Schofield – that was me. You've been looking for me for months and I was standing right in front of you! It was delicious."

"As for Leonard Schofield, he left a bad taste in my mouth. A few nights before I issued that retirement announcement in his name, I snuck into Schofield's house – some big gaudy mansion filled with books by all the scientists he's plagiarized over the years – and I waited for him to come home. But to my surprise, his wife showed up first – who even knew that cantankerous old pervert had enough charm to trick someone into marrying him? I thought about delaying or finding a way to distract her, get her out of the house... but that's when I felt the hunger. This gnawing, not only from my stomach, but seeming to growl from every inch of me, begging to be

fed. I felt like I'd waste away if I didn't consume something. The Flesh was hungry.... I told myself that this end was better for Mrs. Schofield than living another day with that husband of hers. She was about to become part of something greater. I made it quick."

"About an hour later, Schofield came home and his doting wife was there waiting for him. I ate him while wearing his wife's face like a Halloween mask – that made it all the sweeter. In that moment, I let my instinct take over. I let the Flesh take control. My body opened wide into something inhuman... something better... and I pulled the old man into my embrace with a hundred tendril arms until he was enveloped beneath my membrane. Maybe it seemed like he was back in the womb. He struggled, but he was just another weak man, and I felt this surge of ecstasy as his body was digested down to its building blocks and became one with me – one with the Flesh. Not only did I take his meat and his bones, but I felt his memories in my head, his mannerisms in my fingers, like some primal pearl of his personality was now embedded somewhere within me. It was beautiful."

"I spent the next few days wearing his clothes, learning his routine – really becoming the character, you know? Then it was off to the Institute to hand his job over to you, Louisa. Little worker bee Louisa. I hope you stare at every person you pass on the street, every bartender and grad student and janitor for the rest of your life, wondering if it's really me behind their eyes. That's what you deserve."

Audio Log #7 – August 10th 12th

(Research Note: Cassette is dated three days before Dr. Longstreet's package arrived)

"Luce, I'm so sorry for what I said in the last message. Something is terribly wrong inside of me. I thought it was my voice I was hearing in my head,

telling me to do these things — that doesn't make what I've done right, but at least it would've been me making the choices!"

"But over the last few weeks, I feel like my mind is being pushed into the back seat of my own brain — that something else is calling the shots. The hunger. The Flesh. That's who's in command now. I can hear it... or them... I can't tell anymore. It's not just my voice and Schofield's voice, but this shrill chorus of dozens... hundreds of others, crying out from some dark abyss somewhere inside of me, all the time. I wonder if Chayton's voice is in there somewhere."

"It used to just be this itch at the back of my skull, tempting me to give in to my base impulses, and at first it felt good to give it what it wanted. But once I started feeding it, the Flesh began to demand more and to be fed more often. When I hesitated, that's when this... this 'other me' would take over, do the job for me. Recently, it's only been right after I've... digested another person to satiate the hunger that I feel like my own mind can come up for air. That's how I'm recording this right now... I thought that I was the skinwalker, that I was wearing this thing like a mask... but now it feels like the mask is wearing me.

"Luce, if you see me, don't trust me, don't listen to anything I say. Kill me the second you have the chance! Argh!...Go for the heart... Please forgive me!"

Audio Log #8 – Unmarked

"Louisa LaMorte! You bitch! You sneaking little whore! I'm not yours to control! I'm not your little prize to hang over your mantle! YOU CAN'T CONTROL ME! YOU NEVER COULD! WE ARE IMMORTAL! WE ARE UNSTOPPABLE! WE ARE THE FLESH!" (**End Transcript.**)

Professor LaMorte leaned back in her creaky desk chair, rubbing her dry eyes behind her glasses. Dusk had descended on the campus of the Thurston Institute, and after that last haunting audio log, Louisa was checking every shadowed corner for Narissa's eyes. Nothing was impossible now. After sifting through Narissa's logs and field notes, she wasn't sure what to think – had Dr. Longstreet gone insane and just believed she could do all of these horrific, spectacular things? Or were these abilities – these skinwalkers – something real?

Either way, by Narissa's own claim, three people were already dead by her hand, and maybe many more victims of her 'feedings' were still to be discovered. Her best friend was dangerous, of that much Louisa was sure. It wasn't until Louisa stood up to go fetch herself a pot of coffee from the faculty lounge, preparing for a long night of talking to the FBI, that she was stopped dead in her tracks by a sudden realization: Burt had said the package had been hand-delivered. Narissa might still be in the – !

"YAAAAAAAGHHH!" As if on some cruel cue, a scream ricocheted through the labyrinthine halls of the Institute, slicing through the silence of Louisa's office. A man's scream. But who else would be at Thurston so late besides… Dean Braxton!

Louisa bolted from her office, not bothering to slip her sensible shoes back on, instead making a mad barefoot dash towards the Dean's study. As the soles of her feet clapped against the cool marble titles, Professor LaMorte could hear the Dean's cries grow louder, more pained, more animalistic. What had started as a pure masculine yell, like the sound of a wounded soldier, had become a series of moans and shrieks – something altogether more pathetic. By the time Louisa threw open the ornate oaken doors of Braxton's study, the man's cries had turned to pitiful broken whimpers. That's when she saw the Flesh for the first time.

In the center of Braxton's gilded cage of a study, beneath the eyes of bookcase gargoyles and the stern portraits of Deans past, Louisa saw Narissa and Braxton wrapped in an inhuman embrace. Narissa stood behind the Dean, a cobweb of oily sinew spreading out from her spine, sticking to the walls and floor, throbbing with pumps of dark blood, like the beginning strands of some monstrous cocoon.; Tendrils of soggy muscle were wrapped around Braxton's legs and arms, holding him taut like some disfigured scarecrow while Narissa ran her hands across Braxton's face and exposed chest – it looked almost like a lover's caress until Louisa noticed that Narissa's fingers were slipping beneath the skin of Braxton's cheek, wearing the man's face flesh like a silken glove! By this point, Braxton had fallen into a vegetative state, his vacant eyes rolling into the back of his head as his skin boiled from within, his screams now nothing more than a series of involuntary rhythmic gulps that one would hear coming from the throat of a stroke patient in the final throes of a fatal episode.

"Narissa... please," Louisa gasped, barely able to process the horrific sight before her. But in the very corner of her heart, the professor held out hope that some shard of her friend was still in there, fighting against this abomination. But when Narissa turned to face her and Louisa saw the sets of double pupils in each of her misshapen eyes, she knew that she was addressing The Flesh itself.

"Louuuuuiiiisaaaa..." The Flesh spoke in a symphony of dissonant voices. It grinned, flashing rows upon rows of crooked human teeth glinting from the deepest recesses of its mouth. "Ssso glad you could come... to bear witness to Braxton's newwww birrrrth..."

"Let him go, Narissa!" Louisa shouted, her fear mixing with her love to create a potent concoction of courage. "You're killing him!"

"WE ARE FREEING HIM AS WE HAVE BEEN FREED!" The Flesh roared defiantly, its body morphing in tandem with its mounting rage. "All are freed in the embrace of the Flesh!"

"If you're so free, let me speak to Narissa," Louisa demanded, standing her ground.

"You are speaking to her…" The Flesh replied, its voice tinged with an almost childlike confusion, as if it didn't understand the distinction between Narissa and this corrupted amalgamation that she had become. Maybe Louisa was naive to think there even was a distinction – but she wasn't about to give up on Narissa. Not again.

"Narissa, please," Louisa coaxed, keeping her gaze locked on the monster's eyes in an attempt to pierce her words down into its soul, where the Real Narissa was hiding. "Fight this – like you've fought for everything else in your life! I know you, and you're too strong to let this thing win!"

Suddenly, Louisa watched as the creature's pupils dilated, reformed into single human irises and then… a look of recognition! Like a patient emerging from a months-long coma, Narissa stared at Professor LaMorte, shame and terror painting her mangled features.

"Luce," Narissa begged, her voice weak and cracking, as if fighting back tears – or something far more malicious. "God, I'm so sorry. End it, please! End iiiiAAAAYYYEEEE!"

After only a few lucid moments, Narissa's face contorted and spasmed, the very bones of her skull cracking and realigning beneath her thin tarp of her skin. When she looked back at Louisa, the Flesh had regained control – and it was furious.

"WORM!" The Flesh cried out as its body expanded and contorted until it had lost all elements of its humanity, save for a few scattered vestigial limbs that dangled limply from its quivering extremities. It had taken on a shape that was serpentine, alien, something unfathomable – and at the very center of the throbbing skinsack was a black, beating heart. A tentacle of gore shot from the creature's innards and cracked Louisa against the jaw with the force of an oncoming car, sending the Deputy Director careening across the room and slamming into a stand of decorative flags propped up against the study wall.

"WE ARE LOVE! WE ARE PERFECTION! WE ARE THE NEXT STEP ON THE EVOLUTIONARY CHAIN!" The Flesh proclaimed as countless eyes opened across its body, all bloodshot red and blinking as they stared down their prey. "THERE IS ONLY THE FLESH!"

The creature slithered forward with its many tendrils, ready to envelope Louisa in its all-consuming embrace! – until it abruptly stopped short, a sickening squelching sound gurgling out from the Flesh's innards.

Looking down with its many surprised eyes, the Flesh saw a thick wooden pole jutting out from the center of its dark heart as viscous black blood dribbled out of the still-beating organ and onto the pristine study floor. At the other end of the wooden rod was Louisa, her bruised face contorted in a cold grimace – she had taken up one of the broken flags and, using the beast's own momentum against it, had driven the sharp brass flag tip through the Flesh's monstrous heart!

"Butttt... there is only the –," the creature's words were cut short as Louisa thrust the flagpole deeper, sending the metal spiked tip bursting out of the Flesh's back in a shower of shimmering bile. With that final, fatal push, the thing's heart forced out a few last frantic palpitations before finally falling still. Within seconds, its tendrils and webbed membranes melted away into putrid puddles, leaving only the naked body of Narissa Longstreet impaled upon Louisa's spike. It was only when Narissa opened her flittering eyelids that Louisa's battle haze left her and she realized that her hands were covered in her best friend's blood.

"Luce..." Narissa moaned softly, her breaths almost imperceptible as the makeshift spear protruded from her petite chest. But for a moment, Louisa swore she saw a slight grin pass across her friend's face. "Thanks..."

Before she could reply, Louisa watched as Narissa's body boiled away, her bones and her muscles liquifying and slopping down the flagpole into a frothing puddle at the professor's feet.

The police would be called, reports would be filed. Louisa would tell the authorities everything she knew – that Dr. Narissa Longstreet had killed Tokala Fineday and Leonard and Doreen Schofield – but she would conveniently leave out the nature of Narissa's research and choose never to mention the mysterious package that arrived at her door earlier that day. Dean Braxton wasn't dead per say, but his brain was little more than gazpacho by the time the paramedics arrived – and only a few minutes later, representatives from the Thurston Institute barged in and spirited the disfigured Dean away. They claimed to be taking him to a private mental health treatment facility, but no one saw Braxton again after the events of that night.

When Louisa returned to her office to collect her things, it was nearly sunrise. The Institute had offered the traumatized professor a paid leave of absence, as thanks for her quick thinking and selfless actions, but Louisa was too tired to give them an answer. She didn't like the way the men from the Institute had blankly smiled at her, even as the sickening smells from the night's attack still permeated the Dean's destroyed study. Louisa LaMorte did know one thing – she was done with the world of academia, that was for certain.

However, Louisa was destined to finish her ordeal with one more mortifying discovery: when she arrived in her office, she found that Narissa's package, the cassette tapes, and even the tissue used to collect the mysterious glob of membrane from the box edge, were gone!

SIX BLACK BULLETS

It was high noon in the square
Arid tension filled the air
Buzzards cawed and onlookers jawed,
As two figures stood, ready to draw

One man was Leo Dudley, an outlaw of some fame
The other, Bear McElroy, just a boy in search of a name
Out here in the West, many men had met their end
But Bear was desperate to forge his legend.

As the clocktower chimed, shots rang out
Leo had won without a doubt
He had shot the buckle clean off Bear's belt
And Bear's bullet had missed by a mile.

Though Leo hadn't killed him, Bear almost wished he had
For the laughter of the crowd was nearly twice as bad.
"You've got some guts, boy" Leo smirked and spat
"When you're ready for a real duel, you just come on back."

Too embarrassed to show his face, Bear beat it out of town
It wasn't till he reached a crossroads that he stopped to look around
Where did he think he was going? What was he to do?
Bear sighed and dusted off his hat, sure his gunslinger dreams
were through.

But in that moment, he heard a ring
Of tin bells dancing *ding-a-ling*
As a figure approached on a mule-drawn cart
Bear felt a strange chill pass over his heart.

The figure tipped his black brimmed hat
While on his shoulder there sat a red eyed rat
"Leo Dudley made you look like a fool
But you only lost your duel because you lacked the proper tools."

"I'll make you a deal" the black rider reached into his coat
"One of a kind – I don't mean to gloat."
In the palm of his hand, the merchant displayed
Six black bullets – the only six ever made.

"These bullets will strike down any foe
Best any duelist, fast or slow."
Bear stared at the black bullets, eyes wide as could be.
"How on Earth is that possible? And why give them to me?"

"I see that you're destined for a great many things
And it's my passion to give others' dreams wings"
The rider gave him the bullets, but before Bear could pay
The merchant and his donkey were riding away.

Bear returned to challenge Leo again
Leo obliged, cocksure he would win.
But with a black bullet in the chamber of his old Colt piece
Bear shot Leo down and left the outlaw deceased.

While Bear celebrated with whiskey the rest of that day,
He didn't know that his grandmother suddenly passed away
The moment he pulled the trigger, when the clock had rang twelve
By a freak heart attack, Granny McElroy was felled.

With his first bloody win notched on the hilt of his gun
Bear wandered the West in search of the next one
When he gunned down Redd Nichols on a Texas hillside
Back in Ohio, Bear's father keeled over and died.

Four black bullets left, but still Bear didn't know
The price that he paid when he laid a man low.
Across the territory they whispered the young gunslinger's name
So the challenges kept coming – that's the nature of fame.

One day Bear was jumped in a backwater saloon
Nearly stabbed in the back by a fame-hungry goon.
As Bear blew him away, a thug named Benny Cain,
And Bear's beloved brother Tommy was hit by a train.

When he heard the news, Bear's mind fogged with fear
He had used half his black bullets after only a year
As for his family, they were dropping like flies
Each new grave dug brought fresh tears to his eyes.

Maybe it was karma, maybe it was fate
But the convenient timing couldn't be a mistake
Bear thought to hang up his spurs, but retirement wouldn't take
He knew if he quit now, he'd be exposed as a fake!

Bear took it easy for a year or two
Bought himself a homestead, married his wife, Betty Lou
But just when he thought he couldn't want more
Bear heard a familiar jingle outside his front door.

Stepping outside, Bear's fears were confirmed
It was the black hatted merchant, finally returned.
"What do you want?" Bear asked, his voice brave
"I've already paid you your fair share of graves."

"Oh yes you have," he heard the rider agree
"You've become quite the cowboy, all thanks to me.
I see you've retired, but I've come with a test,
An impossible challenge to top all the rest."

"Should you succeed," the shadow man implored
"Your name will live forever, your legacy assured.
Or would you prefer a nobody's life
On this bare patch of country with that plain little wife?"

Bear frowned and looked back
At his humble, dusty shack.
He felt his Colt weigh heavy in the depths of his coat
And a yearning clawing up from the pit of his throat.

"Go to the town of Bandera," the rider commanded
"It is there you'll do battle, as fate has demanded.
You'd better keep those black bullets in your gun."
The merchant winked as he set off against the setting sun.

Reluctant, Bear McElroy did as he was told
To duel one last time, before he was too old
In Bandera he was set upon by three ugly men
They were the O'Terry Gang, just escaped from the pen.

"Bear McElroy" the tallest one spat,
"I've heard the stories about you – any truth to all that?"
"Why don't you find out?" Bear McElroy scowled
"Let's step outside," the three ruffians growled.

Out on Main Street, the sun high above
Bear took his position, said a prayer for his love.
Just one shot rang out as the clock tower chimed
One bullet killed all three gangsters at the same time!

As the O'Terrys fell, Bear's heart swelled with pride
But miles away, poor Betty Lou died
Blood poured from her eyes as her tender brain boiled
And she fell to the floor, her pretty dress soiled.

Yes, Bear McElory had secured his fame
From Shiloh to Chicago, word spread of his devilish aim
Of how a single gunslinger had bested three thugs
But still Bear's revolver cradled one last cursed slug.

Bear was heartbroken to find Betty passed on
He knew it was his fault that his lover was gone.
From that day forth, for twenty-five years,
Bear lived in isolation, alone with his tears.

But legends of the West aren't easily forgot
And still plenty of young guns wanted their shot,
To fell the Great Bear of Bandera on his home turf
To prove to the faceless masses just how much they were worth.

But Bear swore on the day that his Betty died
From his gun that final black bullet never would fly
So he kept his head down, even adopted a cat
But a legacy can't be smothered as easy as that.

One fateful morn, a knocking came at Bear's door
It was a young man with dreams, like Bear years before
He challenged the old gunman and wouldn't listen to "No"

So, revolver in hand, Bear stepped out into the snow.
Out amongst the flurries, as the wind whipped and moaned
Both the duelists stood ready outside of Bear's home
The young man was itching for the shooting to start,
With no appreciation for the gunslinger's art.

But Bear had no intention of firing his gun
He didn't care if the boy shot him, or if the boy won
The black bullets had cost him everyone that he loved
He couldn't send another soul to the heavens above.

As the boy counted down, Bear looked to the West
He saw the black rider watching from a mesa's crest
The cursed merchant grinned – he had finally won
Until Bear aimed his pistol straight up at the sun.

"

NO!" cried the rider as Bear's shot sailed toward the sky

His last bullet was gone in the blink of an eye

Then all of a sudden, the sky turned pitch black

The gunslinger killed the heavens, there was no going back.

TICKETS PLEASE

THREE IN THE MORNING in a suave New York City restaurant might sound glamorous, but when you're slaving away over the back sinks, scrubbing dirty dishes in a sweltering kitchen, the Big Apple charm quickly dissipates. But for Alessandra Martez, this night was just one of many. Despite the grueling graveyard shift, this gig at *L'Entre* had kept her afloat ever since she had moved to New York six months ago – she was "hustling for the dream", or whatever the hell those NYU brats always called it. But for Alessandra, she didn't have a scholarship or rich parents to keep her afloat – her parents were still back in Rio, fighting for every inch. Like her father before her and his father before him, everything Alessandra did was a matter of survival.

But as Alessandra glanced up at the clock above the grill station, she breathed an exhausted sigh of relief – her shift was finally over, at least for tonight. With a few nods and weary goodbyes to the other kitchen staff, Alessandra grabbed what few personal effects she had, clocked out, and ducked out the back door into the alleyway behind the French eatery. The owners always got heated if they saw any of the dishwashers or wait staff exit through the dining room, even at 3 A.M. – something about never wanting patrons to 'see behind the curtain of luxury', but everyone really knew the real reason why. Whatever – a paycheck was a paycheck. Besides, with New York rent as expensive as it was, Alessandra couldn't afford to complain, so she kept her head down as she slipped out the back into the anonymity of the New York night.

As she emerged from the shadowed alleyway and into the neon glow of the 24 hr pizza shops and witching hour bodegas, Alessandra patted herself down to make sure she hadn't forgotten anything in the breakroom – in the black half-apron synched around her waist, she was carrying her wallet, her apartment keys, a creme brulé butane lighter, a wine cork-screw, and a can of *B-Gone* brand pepper spray her mother had sent her as a birthday gift. Her parents were always nervous about her living in a foreign city, but recently, the fears Alessandra had once called unfounded had unfortunately been proven to be valid.

As Alessandra made her way down the dark city sidewalk, she thought of her older brother, Bruno – he had moved to NYC a year before her and disappeared three months after she arrived. Even this late, the streets of New York were still filled with faceless, unsleeping masses, and like she did every night, Alessandra looked into each stranger's eyes, hold-ing out hope that she would one day spot Bruno amongst their ranks.

Alessandra had loved her brother, and back in Brazil they were as close as siblings could be – even despite their four year age gap. Bruno was her protector, her confidant, and her best friend… but she had always known Bruno was troubled, even back in their home country. A year before his move to America, Alessandra had noticed him slipping out of the house to visit the poor favela districts of Rio de Janeiro, disappearing into the shanty town for some covert reason. It wasn't until she walked in on Bruno in his bedroom with a needle in his arm that she realized he was in the grip of heroin abuse.

Her family hoped that Bruno's move to New York, with its change of pace and new set of responsibilities, would help him free himself from his addiction – and for the first few months, they were right. Bruno wrote her letters, telling Alessandra he had gone clean and found a good job –

and eventually, he invited her to come join him in the Big Apple, to get a taste of that good old American prosperity.

But whether this new life had just been a temporary distraction or if he had been lying in his letters the entire time, by the time Alessandra touched down at LaGuardia Airport, she could tell Bruno had returned to his vices. He was gaunt, his eyes constantly wandered, and he always kept his sleeves rolled down over the crux of his arms – Alessandra could infer the rest. For the first few months, she lived with her brother in his Bronx apartment and worked hard, saving up to send Bruno to a hospice or somewhere he could recover… but one night, three months into her time in America, Bruno didn't come home.

Days turned to weeks and Bruno still remained missing, no thanks to the lackluster efforts of the NYPD to locate him. Maybe he had overdosed in some back alley somewhere, or maybe he had fallen into debt with a bad crowd – both the police and their parents assumed the worst, and eventually, even Alessandra began to scan the *New York Post* each morning to see if there were any reports of the body of a Brazilian man washing up on the banks of the Hudson River. Despite her doubts, there was still a spark of hope in Alessandra's heart, and as she wandered through the boulevards of twinkling lights and piss-stained pavement, she dreamed of opening her apartment door to find Bruno sitting on the couch, waiting for her.

But that's all it was – dreaming. Life was unforgiving – plain and simple – and that was one truth that needed no translation between Rio and New York.

Alessandra shook off her late-night musings as she descended the stairs to a subterranean subway station, where she was greeted by a blast of muggy, stale air and an oppressive odor that shocked her back to the present. Good thing too – Alessandra had learned that she had to keep her wits about her in New York's twisting network of train stations. There was a reason she packed light and had done away with her handbags – best not to make yourself a target for the pickpockets and predators that lurked in the corners of one's vision at this time of night. She wore a stony, mirthless expression to dissuade any unwanted interactions, but if some unfortunate still tried to bother her, well, that's what the pepper spray was for.

Despite the reassuring presence of her various armaments, Alessandra released a weary sigh – that blast of torrid air signaled that she had just missed the train, and on the late-night schedule, she knew it would be at least another half hour before another one came along. She collapsed on a bench beside the tracks, listening to the rhythmic echo of the subway cars fade away into the devouring darkness of the spiderweb tunnels – at this rate, it would be gray morning by the time she made it back to the Bronx.

She tossed a glance around the nearly-empty subway station, checking for any nosey MTA workers before she sparked a cigarette – at this time of night, the ticket booths were empty, the adjacent platform was abandoned, and she hoped the NYPD had better things to do than harass smokers and turnstile-jumpers.

As the cigarette crackled between her lips, Alessandra's gaze drifted to the other bench further down the platform where the only other riders were sitting – they were a group of skinny goths, with pale jaundiced skin beneath their spiked leather jackets and the cheap piercings that dotted their features like silver shrapnel. They cackled and shoved each other like a group of high school delinquents, their ridiculous mohawks swaying with each immature jab, their gold capped teeth glinting in the fluorescent lights like shattered glass with each crooked grin.

These guys were grimy punks, gas station vampires out of some gonzo comic book, and Alessandra wanted nothing to do with them – but she had trouble looking away after she noticed there were a few ordinary girls in the midst of the crowd of black leather bozos.

The girls were pretty, in a Long Island sort of way, and certainly didn't fit in with the crust punks around them – the gas station vamps probably picked them up at some bar, judging by how the girls' heads bobbed, slack and tipsy. For those girls, these lowlives might just be a one-night stand destined to be regretted by tomorrow morning, but Alessandra felt a responsibility to keep an eye on them, at least until she reached her stop. None of these Sid Vicious wannabes looked like they weighed more than ninety pounds soaking wet, but that didn't mean that a pack of them couldn't still be dangerous.

Speak of the devil… one of the gutter gremlins had clocked her stare and now he was walking over to Alessandra, his face contorted into a wicked smile. As he drew closer, Alessandra clocked his electric blue mohawk, his Nine Inch Nails t-shirt dotted with cigarette burns, and the smattering of swirling crimson tattoos that clawed their way out from beneath his jacket collar. She didn't have time to consider the ink's artistic implications – by the time she had taken another cigarette drag, the punk was upon her, his dark eyes hungry.

"Hey mama," the punk growled like a tiger emerging from the brush to stare down its prey. "My name's Sebastian, what's yours?"

"None of your business, champ," was all Alessandra said, letting her dispassionate gaze drift forward to communicate to Sebastian that she couldn't be less interested. "Beat it."

"Ooh, bitch's got claws," Sebastian cooed, tossing an amused glance over his shoulder towards his cohorts, not the least bit intimidated. "Probably that hot Latin blood – let's not spill any tonight, eh? You should come hang with me and my boys – we'll show you a good time."

"Oh, a good time like what? Smoking crack in a Sbarros bathroom?" Alessandra replied, her voice frigid and her eyes always directed at the adjacent train platform, never willing to give this creep the satisfaction of a look in the face. "Keep your distance, Vlad, or I'll yank that septum piercing out so hard you'll have to put your nose back together with Scotch tape. Got it?"

"Alright mama, alright. Not our fault you can't have a little fun," Sebastian threw up his hands in mocked surrender, clicking his tongue behind his gray lips as he beat a slow retreat back to his crew's turf. "But you'd better watch that forked tongue of yours, baby – you never know whose feelings you might hurt."

With an extra dose of poison in the final words of his thinly veiled threat, Sebastian returned to his group just as the headlight of an oncoming subway train pierced the darkness of the underground tunnel. Thank God – Alessandra didn't think there'd be another train for at least twenty more minutes, and she didn't want to risk spending any more time alone with these Mad Max cosplayers. The subway train stopped in a peculiar way, with only the last train car opening its doors while the other cars remained dark, their ever-glowing strip lights extinguished. Maybe those cars were being repaired or it was yet another penny-pinching effort by the MTA – Alessandra didn't care, as long as she was that much closer to getting home to her murphy bed.

Much to her chagrin, the gas station vampires and their dates boarded the same train car with her, but she kept her distance by choosing one of the plastic orange seats in the far back, next to the compartment's rear window. There were a few other riders already inside – more pale-faced, party crowd night owls with girls prettier than their pay grade, but none of that was Alessandra's business. Ignoring the weirdos around you was an art every New Yorker was quick to learn and proud to practice.

After another few seconds of watching the gutter punks passing around a dented flask of who-knows-what and lifting it up to their drunken girlfriends' lips with the promises of extending the good time, the train finally began to move forward with a clumsy lurch and the metallic grinding of its weathered wheels. Like listening to a rolling beat on a taut snare drum, the rhythmic *chug-chug-chug-chug* of the subway put Alessandra at ease, and she finally allowed the exhaustion of her long shift to catch up with her. Her sore ankles, the burn on her wrist from a hot skillet – surely the train could outrun her problems until she had regained enough energy to face them tomorrow morning. The only thing that disturbed her feeling of tranquility was the dark subway cars ahead – now that they were deep into the shadowy tunnels beneath Manhattan, it felt as if their train cabin was piloting itself through a void, surrounded by unending, subterranean night. That was until she heard a hiss as the compartment door slid open.

"Tickets, please," announced a conductor in a navy-blue MTA flat-top cap as he began to move through the train car's rowdy passengers. Alessandra expected the punks to give the soft-spoken conductor a hard time, as those types are apt to do in the presence of authority figures, but they quickly handed over their tickets without protest. The conductor didn't bother to check the drunken girls' tickets, either out of a show of good will or a simple lack of interest.

However, as the conductor moved his way back towards Alessandra's corner, she started to panic – she didn't have a ticket! And why would she? Everything was digital now – she used a MetroCard like everyone else. Maybe the machine had been busted at the station or maybe it was some new late-night rule no one had told her about? She also noticed another odd detail: the paper tickets the other passengers were handing over weren't the typical MTA yellow – they were red with a black stripe down the center. Whatever the reason for this bizarre new rule, she didn't know and she didn't have the patience to find out – Alessandra would pay whatever fee she needed to for this interminable night to be over with.

"Tickets, please," the conductor dutifully repeated, looming over Alessandra as she dug through her wallet for her MetroCard, as proof she had made at least some kind of payment.

"Sorry, I don't have a ticket, but I have my–"

"Alessandra?"

Alessandra's head shot up from her lap, the confusion painted across her features soon replaced with true disbelief as she looked into the conductor's eyes to see a familiar face –

"Bruno?"

Standing before her, in the flickering glow of the overhead lights, was her brother, Bruno! A flood of emotion began to erupt from Alessandra's chest, a shocked, unbridled joy catching in her throat as tears welled at the corners of her eyes. Upon first glance, he looked just the same as Alessandra remembered him, his hair tousled the same way, his stubble the same length as it was on the day he disappeared… but the longer she stared, Alessandra started to see past the veil of her disbelief and began to notice that something wasn't right about her brother.

The conductor uniform was strange to be certain, but at first Alessandra could've believed that he had found a new job during his time away – but when she began to notice the corpse blue of his skin, the rot-yellow stain of his fingertips, the flakes of ashen flesh peeling away at the edges of his clothing like dried parchment, she realized Bruno was no longer himself. His eyes were murky, as if they had been replaced with marbles of cracked glass, but deep within their fog, Alessandra could see a deep sorrow in Bruno's gaze.

"Ali," Bruno broke their stunned silence with a sharp, hissing whisper. "What the hell are you doing here?"

"What am I–? What are *you* doing here?" Alessandra stumbled through a retort, thrown off-guard by her brother's less-than-hospitable greeting. "We have to tell Mama and Papa that you're safe–"

"No," Bruno replied, the forcefulness in his voice doing little to mask the fear that Alessandra could detect beneath his words. "We need to get you off this train right now. You're not supposed to be here – it's not safe, not for people like you."

"What do you mean *people like me?*" Alessandra scowled, her patience for her brother's bizarre dance running thin. Was he strung out again? He never talked like this to her before, even when he was doping.

"The living," was all Bruno had the chance to say before all the strip lights in the subway car suddenly turned from their typical harsh fluorescent white to a deep, all-encompassing red, reflecting off each glinting strip of exposed metal and mixing with the inky shadows from the tunnel outside to create a hellish kaleidoscope. Above the compartment door Bruno had entered through, a crimson symbol – a crooked glyph from some alien language – sizzled as it scorched itself into the metal of the doorframe, just as the familiar *ding-dong* that prefaced the MTA's typical intercom announcements echoed through the train's speakers.

The gutter punks looked around, their sneering smiles growing sickeningly wide as a robotic voice reverberated through the tin can train car:

"Welcome, valued travelers. This is an express outbound train, making no stops until the End of the Line," the saccharine animatronic voice announced, its message distorted by small bursts of static interference. "Remember to please stay confined to your train car for the duration of our trip, both for your safety and the safety of our crew."

"Feeding may commence," the announcement decreed, much to the snarling satisfaction of the train compartment's other inhabitants. "Welcome aboard the Nocturne Express."

As one final chime echoed through the subway's speakers, Alessandra watched in horror as the leather-clad gutter punks reared their heads back and let out a combined animalistic shriek that reverberated through the metal tube at a nauseating, inhuman frequency. Beneath the crimson flickers of light emanating from the spastic fluorescents overhead, the gas station vampires lived up to their name as their eyes rolled back into their skulls and the pale skin at the corners of their lips were torn asunder, leaving behind deep, bloodless gashes and revealing mouths full of jagged teeth and primordial fangs.

Without a moment of hesitation, the ravenous punks descended upon their dates, tearing into the smooth skin of the women's necks, ripping into arteries and snapping the poor girls' spines like bloodthirsty hounds thrashing helpless rabbits between their jaws. Their victims were unable to do anything more than let out a chorus of gurgling moans before falling deathly still.

"What the hell are they –?" Alessandra murmured in a state of petrified shock, watching as the gutter punks filleted the bodies of their dates with canine teeth and distended, yellowed claws. It was as if these creatures had never been fed before in their lives, and now they were consumed by the need to satiate their impossible hunger.

"We have to go, now!" Bruno commanded, grabbing his sister's hand. His grip sent a graveyard chill through Alessandra's body, but she didn't have much of a choice – with only endless darkness speeding by outside the train's back door, the only way out was through.

"Got something to defend yourself?" Bruno asked as he yanked Alessandra to her feet and pulled a long-necked silver flashlight from his conductor's belt, holding it at the ready. "Alessandra?"

"I – Yes," Alessandra shook herself out of the maelstrom of internal dread that had begun to consume her mind and reached into her apron pocket to grab her wine corkscrew. She gripped the piece of metal restaurantware tight between her knuckles, the twisted tip protruding from her fist like makeshift brass knuckles.

"Don't think, just focus on making it through that door," Bruno instructed – despite his deadened white eyes, Alessandra still found some comfort in her brother's gaze. Turning her eyes to the end of the train car, she saw Sebastian and his blue mohawk standing right beside the door, tearing blood drenched flesh from a shattered skull. Her eyes narrowed as Alessandra found her fear supplanted by a new fuel – the fire of hate. The power of pure human survival.

The siblings burst forward from the rear of the train car, the sounds of their pounding footfalls waking the frenzied creatures from their feeding fit. With devilish hisses scratching out from behind their gnashing teeth and coal-black tongues, the punks leapt towards the pair – only to be greeted by a blinding blast of white light from Bruno's flashlight!

As the powerful cone of what Alessandra could only describe as distilled daylight found its mark – a crust punk with pink-tipped spiked hair and a thick lip ring – the creature's skin began to smolder and burn like flaming parchment, reducing half the monster's face to gray dust. The pink-haired punk collapsed backward, clawing in agony at his warped skull, now revealed from beneath his disintegrating skin. Even just hearing the monster's cries made Alessandra nauseous, but this was not a time for hesitation.

Even as they watched their comrade writhe in a fit of searing pain, the other bloodsuckers still leapt forward, hoping to overpower the conductor and his daylight deluge – but the Martez siblings refused to be overrun.

Fighting back-to-back as they had fought against the bullies and belligerents on the streets of Rio in their youth, Alessandra and Bruno repelled the hungry ones. Alessandra skewered one skinhead through the neck with her corkscrew as he pounced towards her while Bruno jammed his flashlight through another creature's eye sockets and ignited the bulb, burning a hole through the back of the emaciated beast's head. But even as they fought valiantly against impossible odds, more glinting rows of teeth and blood-crusted claws took the place of the fallen – Alessandra knew that they were fighting on borrowed time.

"Go for the door, now! I'm right behind you," Bruno shouted over the hellish snarls and wails of anguish that now filled the subway car. After clubbing an oncoming punk with the hilt of his flashlight, Bruno used its beam to cut a pathway of daylight through the hoard of predators, deatomizing hands and scorching undead flesh as he flung his sister forward. Just as Alessandra burst through the crowd of emaciated attackers and reached a hand for the sliding door, her shot at salvation was interrupted by Sebastian, his spiked leather now spattered with slick blood and his serpentine jaw dripping with gore as it curled into a cruel sneer.

"Heyyy mama," Sebastian growled with a guttural rumble, his black eyes consumed by a primordial craving. "Told ya you shouldn't have hurt my feelings!"

With a bestial roar, the mohawked monster swiped at Alessandra, Sebastian's crooked claws finger their mark in the soft tissue of Alessandra's shoulder and soaking her white button-up with blood. The claws dug deep into her muscles, trapping the young woman only inches away from Sebastian's rancid maw.

"I could smell that hot blood from blocks away… and you walked right into our subway station," Sebastian cackled, his slithering black tongue slinking out from between his teeth and lapping up the warm blood pumping from Alessandra's wound. "Deep down, there's a part of you that wanted this."

"I didn't think you could get any less charming…" Alessandra groaned, grimacing through her pain just long enough to shove her wine corkscrew into Sebastian's eye, so deep that she felt the bent corkscrew tip scratch the bone at the rear of his socket! The leader of the gutter punks staggers backward, his menacing growl replaced with a high-pitched wail as he clawed at the spike protruding from his gaunt face – leaving the train car door wide open.

"Bruno, now!" Alessandra barked over her shoulder as she flung the door open, the whipping wind from the subway tunnel battering her face.

With another blast from his flashlight, Bruno burst past the talons and teeth of the pack of punks and the siblings crashed through the compartment door into the walkway between train cars. Gripping her limp, bloodied shoulder, Alessandra scrambled to her feet and slammed the door shut just in time to watch Sebastian pull the corkscrew from his mangled eye. The burning glyph above the doorway glowed with a scalding heat as the train car sealed itself again.

"You still think quick on your feet, *irmã*," Bruno breathed a shallow sigh of relief as he pulled himself off the gangway floor, holding a length of clinking chain to steady himself as the subway train rocked to and fro. However, Alessandra was not as amused, and as her adrenaline settled, questions returned to the forefront of her mind.

"What the hell was all that, Bruno?" Alessandra grimaced as she did her best to stop her shoulder's bleeding. "Those punks – they tore into those girls! They were inhuman… And you! Where the hell have you been? I've been looking for you for months, you asshole! And you've been doing what – playing *Thomas the Tank Engine* down here?"

"I've been dead, Ali," Bruno replied, his voice grim and deadly sober. Taken aback by such a blunt decree, Alessandra gazed down at her brother, for the first time clocking the injuries he sustained in the train car brawl. His pristine conductor's uniform was sullied with claw marks, and his pallor skin was marred with gashes… and from those gashes poured not blood, but trickling streams of silver sand that twinkled on the subway tunnel wind like lost flecks of starlight. "And those things back there, you can call them ghouls, vampyr – whatever you like. They feed on blood and they hate the daylight – that's the important part. But hopefully we won't have to deal with them from here on out."

"Those glyphs above the doors, they keep the passengers sealed in their train cars," Bruno explained, looking back through the door window just as Sebastian tried in vain to pry the door open, but only succeeded in burning his clawed hands on the glyph's supernatural surface. No matter how much frothing and snarling Sebastian did, he wasn't breaking through. "They're old glyphs though, so I can't promise they'll hold forever."

"You're saying all this shit like it makes sense," Alessandra sighed, pursing her brow between her quaking fingers. "You're not dead, you're standing right here in front of me!"

"No. I'm standing on the Nocturne Express – so are you, so you'd better get used to it," Bruno shook his head – he clearly wasn't thrilled about the situation either but diluting the truth wasn't going to help anyone.

"This isn't one of the MTA's late-night lines, if you haven't already pieced that together. This train runs on impossible tracks, carrying all sorts of darkness from beyond into the mortal world each night to feed and then ferrying them back to their domain before the dawn – a place they call the End of the Line. You wonder why New York City is such a weird, messed up city? Why there's nowhere else like it anywhere in the world? It's because this whole goddamn place is a supernatural beacon – a waystation for the things that go bump in the night."

"For just a few minutes each night, the veil between worlds is thin enough that regular people can see the Nocturne Express... even climb aboard if they don't know any better," Bruno continued as he ripped free a length of his tattered sleeve and began to wrap it around Alessandra's wound, exposing the mummified corpse-skin beneath his clothes. "That's part of the train's design. Stragglers, the homeless, junkies – we become snacks for these things on their ride home. If you don't get torn apart by one of the nightmares in these train cars, the Railmaster will find you and turn you into a Shade – not quite alive, not quite dead, cursed to serve the train on its endless, bloody commute."

"That's what happened to you, isn't it?" Alessandra asked, her tone softening as the pain in her brother's voice pierced like a needle into her heart.

"I wandered into the wrong station at the wrong time... what can you do?" Bruno said with a shrug and a forlorn smile. "I tried to find my way back to you, I really did..."

"I know... I know you did," overcome with emotion and making a noise somewhere between a whimper and a chuckle, Alessandra wrapped her arms around her brother's neck and pulled him into the kind of tight embrace reserved only for family. Even as Bruno's skin crackled like rotted wood and his bones creaked like rusted subway pipes, Alessandra held him close, as if refusing to let him go ever again. "I'm going to get both of us out of here, okay?"

Bruno burrowed his face into his sister's shoulder with a forlorn look in his eyes, but when the hug finally ended, all he said was: "We have to get you off before the train reaches the End of the Line. And that means making our way to the Driver at the front of the train."

"How far is that from here?" Alessandra asked, putting aside her sentimentality as she steeled herself for whatever harrowing journey lay ahead.

"The Nocturne has five compartments – that means we've got four cars to go," Bruno replied, taking a frayed handkerchief from his back pocket and holding it over his nose and mouth. "Still have Dad's bandana?"

"Yeah – never go on shift without it," Alessandra nodded, producing a maroon bandana from her back pocket – a gift from her father when she moved stateside. Following Bruno's example, she covered her mouth, taking in a nostrilful of food aromas from her restaurant shift, savoring the leftover scraps of the waking world.

"When we get into the next train car, keep the bandana over your face, don't talk and don't breathe. These guys rely on sound to hunt and they're fairly docile if they're not provoked," Bruno explained as he neared the next compartment door, preparing to slide it open for his sister. "Honestly, I've got more of a right to be scared of these guys than you do."

"Why's that?" Alessandra cocked an eyebrow as she reached her free hand into her apron to arm herself, her fingers finding the pepper spray can in the corner of her pocket – after all, she had left her corkscrew embedded in Sebastian's face.

"If there's one thing these next passengers like more than living prey, it's dead flesh," Bruno growled with contempt as he slid the door open. "Be careful."

Alessandra nodded as she stepped across the dark threshold in front of her, entering the dimly lit train car as silently as her wounded body could muster. As Bruno filed in behind her, Alessandra scanned the space – unlike the modern MTA style of the first car, Alessandra noticed that this compartment looked vintage, as if it had been plucked from one of the grimy elevated trains that had once crisscrossed New York back in the dirty 70s. The dented metal compartment was lit by a few weak bulbs, painting its inhabitants' shadowed silhouettes in a sickly green light as the train rumbled along its midnight tracks.

The silhouettes looked human as far as Alessandra could tell, but they were all dressed in long, out-of-season trench coats and wide-brimmed fedoras and pork pie hats, each figure deathly silent save for an unnerving white noise that seemed to permeate the entire compartment.

With an encouraging nod from Bruno, Alessandra began to slowly make her way through the train car, her brother following close behind as a hum permeated the space. Even through the bandana, she could still smell the sickly-sour, acidic odor that wafted through the compartment, coming from the slick, oily film that seemed to cling to every surface in sight. As she inched her way past the first trenchcoated figure, the man – or whatever he was – didn't flinch or acknowledge her presence in any way, but as she neared his sleeve, the humming noise became a shrill buzzing that made Alessandra's skin crawl and seemed to vibrate the very marrow in her bones. But she kept moving and the siblings made their way through the rumbling train car untouched – until the Nocturne Express hit a bump in the tracks.

As the subway curved around a bend in the tunnel, the train car jostled and swayed wildly, sending Alessandra and Bruno scrambling for whatever balance they could muster – Bruno was able to catch himself on one of the commuter poles lining the center of the compartment, but Alessandra was not so lucky. Thrown by the train's sudden redirection, Alessandra was sent crashing into one of the sticky metallic seats with a hideous clang, cracking a rib and clipping one of the passengers' shoulders on her way down. Before the sound of her impact had even finished reverberating through the metal tube, all of the silhouettes turned towards Alessandra, their eyeless faces focusing on the girl's wheezing even as she tried to smother her pained groans with her bandana.

But it was too late to hide – the buzzing had increased in its volume and veracity and now each silhouette growled with the sounds of a great swarm, combining into the roar of an enraged hornet's nest. As the figure closest to her stepped into the glow of the emerald light bulbs, Alessandra finally saw underneath his clothes – beneath his wilted hat and stained longcoat was not a human man made of flesh and blood, but instead a writhing swarm of insects, coalesced into a vague human shape as the bugs crawled overtop one another in a ravenous, slithering mass. The figure's shoulder that she collided with on her way down now hung limply as a chittering stream of cockroaches and centipedes dripped out of the empty coat sleeve, scattering across the oily train car floor and skittering toward Alessandra's exposed ankle.

As if cued by some silent hive mind, the other insectoid passengers began to converge on Alessandra, leaving wriggling trails of silverfish and ant colonies in their wake, grating screeches and mouthless moans echoing from their silhouettes as they descended upon the wounded waitress. Just as Alessandra could feel the pinpricks of insectoid legs climbing up her pants and mandible fangs sinking into her flesh, a sudden noise drew the attention of the entire train car:

"HEY! OVER HERE!" Bruno shouted at the far end of the compartment as he banged his flashlight rod against one of the metal poles, commanding the attention of writhing masses. As if receiving new orders from whatever unseen master they served, even the insects feasting on Alessandra slithered back to their host bodies as their hunger was redirected towards the undead conductor. The allure of Bruno's delicious, decayed flesh was too strong for these mindless beings to resist.

"No!" Alessandra gasped, but a stern glare from Bruno swiftly silenced her – 'Make this worth it', he seemed to say with his eyes. Pushing her tears down and keeping her head low, Alessandra began to crawl toward the door at the far end of the train car on her hands and knees, careful not to collide with any of the shambling masses as they converged on her brother.

"You want a feast, you scavenger bastards? Come on then!" Bruno called out, making as much of a racket as possible to mask the sounds of Alessandra's panicked retreat across the slick steel floor. Reaching down and digging his gray fingernails to his brittle wrist, Bruno peeled back the flaking flesh from the bone of his forearm, revealing the tendons of necrotic muscle and broods of maggot larvae beneath – all delicacies to these vermin.

Shedding their facsimile of human clothing, the insectoid men descended upon Bruno with the sickening sounds of crunching exoskeletons and thrashing mandibles as they tore into his wilted limbs and his dead flesh in an all-encompassing swarm. But even as roaches crawled into his eyes and colonies of blowflies invaded his chest cavity, devouring his innards from the inside out, no pain registered on Bruno's face – he just kept his gaze on his sister, giving her the last ounces of silent encouragement he could muster as she reached the train car door. But Alessandra was not built for such coldness, and as she watched her brother's face decay beneath the feeding frenzy, she felt an instinctual cry escape her throat:

"BRUNO!" Alessandra wailed as tears streamed down her raw cheeks, her back pressed against the compartment door as she fought against the despair that sought to overtake her. It had only been a few precious minutes since she had been reunited with her brother and she didn't know if her heart could bear losing him a second time.

"Go...," Bruno's voice slurred as his vocal chords were devoured – but even in this haunting moment, his skull now half-exposed and his demise imminent, her brother still found the strength to muster one last smile for Alessandra before he was pulled under the sea of insects for the last time.

As her cry attracted the attention of the closest trench coat roaches, Alessandra's mind kicked into a survivalist haze – and before she knew it, she was holding her arms out in front of her, pepper spray in one hand and her butane lighter in the other. Clicking both triggers at the same time, Alessandra ignited the aerosol spray, engulfing the two closest insect hordes in a blast of pepper spice fire! But even as the man-like amalgamations crumbled away into piles of charred cockroach shells and withered worm carcasses, the bugs that survived soon reformed into a new being, just as hungry as their smoldering predecessors. Alessandra had bought herself a few seconds, but as she saw Bruno disappear beneath an all-consuming mass of flailing legs and glinting bug eyes, she knew her brother was gone.

Willed on by some subconscious force of self-preservation, Alessandra backed through the train car door and slammed the metallic slab closed behind her just as a black mass of blowflies and locust slammed into the small porthole window. The ravenous swarm piled against the glass like an ancient plague blotting out the sun, having been only milliseconds shy of reaching their living prey. With an almost patronizing chime, the jade green glyph above the doorway reconstituted itself, and for at least a few precious moments, Alessandra was safe.

She slid down the door, collapsing onto the rocking gangway between train cars as her body was wracked with frantic sobs. Like a child who had lost their guardian in some foreign, chaotic place, Alessandra refused to go any further – she would rather curl up and die right here on the open tracks than face another round of horrors without her brother by her side.

But remembering back to what Bruno had said – about the Railmaster, the Shades, the End of the Line – Alessandra knew that a fate far worse than death awaited her if she gave up the fight now. She would make Bruno's sacrifice worth it, and not just by making it off this train alive – she would derail the Nocturne Express for once and for all.

A new vengeful heat ignited in her belly, Alessandra threw open the door to the next train car with no way of knowing what awaited her on the other side. Immediately upon opening the door, Alessandra was assaulted by the stench of decay and feces, as if she had just stepped foot into a rural pig stye in the middle of this metropolitan subway tunnel. As her eyes adjusted to the dark compartment, illuminated by a single hanging lamp that swayed with each bump and bend in the train's path, she realized her barnyard comparison was not far off – the walls of this car were lined with rows upon rows of rusty steel cages, lined with rotting tufts of straw and the sloppish remains of whatever meager meals had been fed to the prisoners within. As she listened past the sounds of metal wheels grinding across warped tracks, she began to hear a host of distorted animal cries, like a zoo descending into madness during the chaos of some biblical thunderstorm.

But Alessandra had little time to gain her bearings or attempt to identify the shifting shapes within the cage, be they human or something far worse – because as soon as she turned her attention back to towards the door at the opposite end of the compartment, she was greeted by a massive shadow standing before her that hadn't been there a just moment before. The silhouette was hulking and misshapen and it raised some sort of horrible club above its head, gripped between its meaty, bandaged fingers.

But as the shape neared, she realized it was not a club in its hands, but instead a grime-stained axe, clumsily affixed to what appeared to be a human femur with a cacophony of rusted nails and blood-caked barbed wire. Barely giving her time to raise her arms in self-defense, the figure brought its weapon down on Alessandra, where it found its mark in the thin tissue between her middle and ring fingers! The horrific blade split her hand down the center with such carnal violence that her fingers and palm were reduced to little more than mangled strands of meat and bone, the two halves of her once-dominant hand dangling uselessly in the night air like a bloodied banana peel.

When the shadowed berserker yanked the blade back out of Alessandra's brutalized limb, a spurt of black blood came with it… and even through her screaming agony and the haze of shock, Alessandra swore that she watched her attacker lick the blood from the soiled blade before he cracked her in the face with the hulking bone handle, knocking her unconscious.

When Alessandra came to, her mind parting the dark fog that might signal a concussion, she couldn't be sure if only minutes or hours had passed – down in these sunless tunnels, the Nocturne Express seemed to be shrouded in an endless night. She must have been unconscious for a while, seeing as when she awoke, Alessandra found herself locked in one of the train car's many cramped cages and her right hand bandaged with a soiled strip of gauze. Even though the bandages helped to keep her fingers together, she could barely feel anything below the wrist – her hand was little better than dead weight at this point. Her digits were so numb that it took a second or two for Alessandra to notice that her pinky finger was missing.

As she stirred awake, Alessandra banged her already sore skull against the roof of her cage, quickly discovering that her new confinement was too small for her to even sit up – she had to lay on her stomach, like a wounded animal awaiting its master's mercy. However, Alessandra wasn't about to just wait around to be used as livestock or some perverted pet by her jailer – she began to scan the compartment, centering her scrambled mind as she started to formulate an escape plan.

Just like the last train car, this one also appeared to be unstuck from time, its wood paneled walls and wrought iron accoutrements giving it the appearance of some ancient locomotive from the barbaric days of the Old West. Above her, rows of blood-rusted hooks hung from the ceiling, swaying side to side and clanking against each other like menacing windchimes, calling out for more meat. But Alessandra couldn't spend long considering those implications, as the sounds of sloppy mastication brought her attention back to her jailer.

Across the train car sat her captor, straddled atop a crooked stool in front of a crackling coal burning furnace in the center of the compartment, stoking the licks of flame inside as his monolithic axe sat propped against the furnace's iron facade. In the light of the furnace, Alessandra could finally make out the homunculus' features: he appeared to be a man, but he was impossibly obese and sported bizarre proportions, his engorged arms hanging down at his sides like a putrid gorilla. Beneath the shreds of leather hide that he must've considered to be clothing, Alessandra could see the inflamed whip scars and claw marks that dotted the man's pale skin – a history of torture and retribution painted across his very flesh. Atop the man's head, he sported a leather shawl that hung down over most of his face like an executioner's hood pulled from the dungeons of some medieval keep – and judging by his imposing form and sickening bloodlust, Alessandra figured this man would've been more at home splitting skulls on the bloody fields of Europe a thousand years ago.

As she squinted through the darkness, searching for her tormentor's face, Alessandra was horrified to realize that her captor did not have the mouth of a man beneath the contours of his leather hood – instead, a filth-flecked pig's snout protruded from the man's skull, twisted, gore-caked tusks protruding up from the edges of his gluttonous mouth, curling his engorged lips into a bloated, filthy smile. As for the sounds of mastication that had drawn her attention to the looming Swine in the first place, Alessandra saw he was sucking on something slender and fleshy, like a drunkard sucking the meat off of a barroom chicken wing… it didn't take long for her to recognize the small butterfly tattoo inked into the side of his midnight snack. She had gotten that same butterfly tattooed on the inside of her pinky finger just before she left Brazil.

Alessandra turned her head away, her stomach doing somersaults as she fought back the urge to vomit in her dog crate of a cell. Even though she could barely feel her hand anymore, watching that bastard chew on her digit, she could still feel the phantom pain of the meat slopping off her bones. Instead, Alessandra turned her eyes to the cages beside her to see what other captives the Swine had locked away. She seemed to be the only pure human in the place, but there was an entire Noah's Ark of bizarre monsters and animal experiments groaning from their cells. There were more terrestrial animals like twenty-foot-long serpents and a few of NYC's famed albino alligators, alongside more mutated creatures like two-headed bat-winged monkeys and eyeless, spider-legged mutts, all horrifically stitched together with a childlike curiosity by their piggish captor's merciless needle.

In the cage directly next to her, Alessandra heard not gnashing teeth or rumbling growls, but the whimper of a wounded child. As the furnace flame threw flickering firelight into the neighboring cell, Alessandra saw the twisted form of what she could only describe as a 'rat-boy' – it was the size of a ten-year-old child, with a mangled assortment of human arms and rodent hind legs, skin peppered with patches of matted gray fur, with a rat's nose protruding from what had once been a human skull. He was like some P.T. Barnum sideshow creation brought to life. But what really cut Alessandra to her core was the rat child's soft, distinctly human eyes, red and brimming with fear – they reminded her of Bruno's eyes after their father scolded him as a boy.

"Hey… it's going to be okay," Alessandra whispered to the rat-boy, careful not to let their jailer hear her. At first the rat-boy hissed, startled by this sudden noise from the hairless woman in the cell beside him, but just like a stray cat warming up to a stranger with a bowl of food, the rodent child soon calmed and inched towards the edge of its cage, closer to Alessandra.

"I'm going to get you out of here," Alessandra was unsure if the pitiful creature could even understand her reassurances, but it was clear that this rat child hadn't heard kindness in a person's voice in a long time, if ever. As

Alessandra reached out a hand towards her fellow captive to pet the poor creature, a searing jolt of electrical energy shot through her body upon contact with the steel cage bars – their pens were electrified!

The sudden shock forced an involuntary yelp out of Alessandra, finally drawing the Swine's attention. The hulking monster rose from his seat, the miniscule pinpricks of light glinting from beneath his leather hood telling Alessandra that the hog's beady eyes were now upon her. Tossing the scraps of Alessandra's pinky bone to the ground and snorting out a few powerful gusts of noxious air from his deformed snout, the Swine began to approach her cell. He dragged his axe behind him like a felled tree trunk in the hands of some giant, the nauseating sound of metal grinding on metal echoing through the train car as the soiled blade scrapped across the train floor. Upon reaching her cage, the Swine bent down, his rotund form folding into itself as he brought himself face-to-face with Alessandra – this close, she could smell the rot on his breath and the awful combination of sour sweat on old leather. She could see a few tendons of errant finger flesh hanging from the pig-man's tusks.

For a moment, the Swine said nothing and did nothing, watching her like a demented child staring at the fish they won at the county fair. Then, it raised one sausage finger to its cauliflower lips and issued a hissing *shush* along with a cavalcade of squeals, as if laughing at her. But thankfully, the Swine didn't have the time to do much else as the train car door was suddenly flung open and a looming figure entered.

"Swine," the figure spoke in a raspy voice echoing from a lungless throat. "Back away from the girl. She is not yours to toy with."

Much to Alessandra's surprise, the Swine snorted and backed away instantly upon hearing this figure's command. As the silhouette stepped into the firelight, Alessandra realized that this man did not cast a shadow… because he himself was a walking shadow. The man appeared to be dressed in a black duster coat and a dark conductor's cap – similar to the one Bruno had worn, but clearly denoting this man as a higher stature than her brother – but there was no face beneath the hat's brim. Instead, the figure's clothing, his body, and his face were all constructed from a roiling mass of smoke and shadows, with only a set of blazing white eyes shining out from the rippling maelstrom.

As the shadow figure walked, his feet made no contact with the floor, floating unabated through the space as if gliding across a sleek stretch of ice. When he passed in front of the furnace's flaming mouth, Alessandra realized that this figure was translucent, the flickering of the firelight permeating his body like muffled sunbeams through a thick curtain.

She had no way to be sure, but Alessandra was certain that this was the Railmaster Bruno had spoken of – the man who had turned her brother into a Shade. Alessandra made a promise to herself that she would kill this Railmaster before the night was through.

"She must pay the debt her brother left vacated," the Railmaster decreed, his voice and inflection never shifting from a state of abject dispassion – such was the nature of a heartless being like this shadow man. "One thousand years to be served upon the Nocturne's rails. One thousand years of walking betwixt the shadows is to be her fate. You have done enough damage already, Swine – I will not have you stitching her into one of your monstrosities."

The hog-man squealed in an animalistic protest but was soon silenced by a touch from the shadow conductor. The moment just one of the Railmaster's black fingers touched the Swine's pig flesh, a deathly chill passed over the beastmaster's body as the color was sapped from his veins, as if being seized by rigor mortis right then and there. Perhaps showing an ounce of mercy – or more likely because he needed the Swine alive to serve some twisted purpose – the Railmaster released his grip on the pig-man and the lifeblood returned to the Swine's arm. That had only been a warning, the reward for insubordination aboard the Nocturne Express.

"I will return for the girl once we have reached the End of the Line," the Railmaster whispered like steam from a cracked pipe. "Until then, she is not to be harmed."

As the Swine nodded and wept, still clutching his cursed arm, the Railmaster retreated back through the train car door, becoming one with the all-encompassing darkness as he disappeared. The entire time, the spectral conductor had never looked towards Alessandra once, as if her subjugation was all but certain. But maybe the Railmaster should have looked, because as he had been disciplining his piggish underling, Alessandra had been hard at work.

While the Swine had been distracted, Alessandra had studied the electrified cages and noticed that they were all connected on the same circuit, each pen linked to the next by a series of tangled wires. But it seemed that the brutish beastmaster was not the best maintenance man – the frayed wires had been hastily patched and soldered together, leaving vulnerable points of exposed wires exposed beneath the haphazard duct tape and their shredded rubber casings. One good surge would short out the entire system, and Alessandra was confident that her oafish captor didn't have the foresight to install a circuit breaker.

Clutching her apartment keys between the managed knuckles of her bandaged right hand, Alessandra wrapped her arm with her apron in the hopes of adding a little extra insulation. She knew this plan was going to hurt one way or another, but at this point in her nightmarish evening, a little more pain was just a drop in the bucket if that meant taking these monsters down with her. With a reassuring glance towards the frightened rat-boy and one more look out the train car window to make sure the Railmaster's white eyes were gone, Alessandra jammed her keys into the exposed wiring!

As volts of electricity surged through her body, Alessandra watched as the electronic panels on each of the cages overloaded in explosive showers of sparks that startled the disoriented Swine, sending the lumbering warden tumbling backwards to the compartment floor like an overturned turtle. Finally pulling her arm back as she wrestled for control of her palpitating heart rate, Alessandra watched as each cage lock disengaged and the doors slid open, the Swine's monsters emerging from their captivity with carnivorous eyes dead set on their former master. The little rat-boy gave her a grateful look before his eyes turned dark, slinking out from his cell to join his experimental brethren as they descended upon their creator.

As Alessandra limped her way out of the Swine's pen, she grabbed one of the steel meat hooks from its dangling resting place – it wasn't ideal, but she was out of weapons and down a hand, so it would have to do. She didn't know how she was going to kill the Railmaster with a bit of curved metal, but she'd figure something out. As she slid the cabin door open, she could hear the Swine's last pathetic oinks and pained squeals before he was drowned out by the animalistic cries of his many pets as they used the corrupted bodies he had given them to tear the pig-man apart, limb by revolting limb. After all, every pet deserves a treat now and then.

Alessandra left the train door open as she passed through, this time leaving the glyph unsealed. The Swine's animal captives had been jailed against their will for too long – who was she to stop them from slipping off into Manhattan's subterranean tunnels, to live out the rest of their short lives in a modicum of peace? New York had enough boogeymen that few more poor souls wouldn't be noticed. She took her time crossing the swaying gangway between train cars – with only one good hand to help her balance, she had to play it safe. She hadn't come this far just to be dashed beneath the Nocturne's wheels only two compartments away from freedom.

Using the chain link railing to steady herself, the weary waitress reached the next door, pausing for a moment as she noticed an azure glow emanating from the porthole window. When she slid the door open, Alessandra came face to face with the source of the dazzling sapphire light.

The engine room was almost alien compared to the rest of the train – the compartment was constructed from flawless black steel, polished to an impossible sheen and without a single bolt or welding scar to show for its construction, as if Alessandra had stepped into a hall of mirrors reflecting the night sky in upon itself. At the heart of the chamber was exactly that – the heart of the Nocturne Express. Its engine was a massive machine, crisscrossed by a labyrinth of pipes and pistons, blasts of steam erupted from its many valves.

But what drew Alessandra's gaze like a moth to a lantern flame was the mouth of the engine – where in an earthly train one might find a black gated iron maw filled with piles of burning charcoal, the Nocturne engine's hatch was wide open and blazed with supernatural tongues of blue and white flames, the light from the inferno shimmering like a polar aurora rather than glowing like ordinary embers. Taking a few steps closer to the mouth of the engine, Alessandra was stunned to realize that the sounds of crackling of coals had been replaced with an eerie chorus of moans and wails, murmuring and muffled as if crying out from some void far away. Venturing even closer, Alessandra peered into the seemingly bottomless engine and into the azure blaze, but reeled back when she began to see thousands of screaming human faces dancing in the unearthly fire, their expressions of anguish flickering in and out of existence in rhythm with the roiling tongues of flame.

"The Soul Engine is a thing of beauty, is it not?" a raspy voice spoke from the shadows. Alessandra whipped around, meat hook at the ready. But to her dismay, she soon realized that the voice was not echoing from one shadowed corner of the engine room, but instead from every shadow, all around her.

"It is a wonder that no mortal has ever beheld. Even your brother never made it this far – that is to say when a living heart still beat within his chest," The Railmaster seemed to mock her, though his voice never changed. Stepping out from behind the Soul Engine's hulking frame, the Railmaster emerged from the darkness, coalescing the very shadows around him into what passed for a physical form. "But now your brother knows full well the majesty of this engine's heart. He has been shown the glory firsthand."

As if cued by the Railmaster's taunts, Alessandra recognized a familiar cry from within the flames, and watched as Bruno's face appeared amongst the countless other sacrifices, calling out to her for the briefest moment before being swallowed by the spectral inferno once again.

"I'll kill you for that," Alessandra grimaced, tightening her grip on the meat hook and readying a swing. She had no plan, no hope to speak of – but she wasn't leaving this compartment until the Railmaster was dead.

"You'll do nothing, child," the Railmaster hissed with a voice like wind growling through the trunk of a dead willow tree.

As Alessandra swung the heavy metal hook, the phantom conductor's black form simply floated through her attack and through Alessandra's body itself! Feeling a crippling chill pass through her muscles as the air was forcibly ripped from her lungs, Alessandra collapsed to her knees, her hook clattering uselessly across the engine room floor.

"The living are so preoccupied with their own individuality. Your kind have diluted yourselves into believing that you are special, simply because you were given the barest spark of life. You each believe yourselves to be an extraordinary exception – yet that defies the very nature of the extraordinary, does it not," The Railmaster soliloquized, his long shadow loomed above Alessandra as she gasped for breath. "But after spending eons stoking the flames of this holy engine, I have learned a singular truth – the living are nothing more special than fuel."

"I've made it this far – I'd say that's pretty special," Alessandra spat, turning a fearless gaze up towards the shadow man. "My brother freed himself from your control – I'd say that's pretty special too. You're just a parasite."

Though the Railmaster's face was composed of living darkness, Alessandra swore she could see a look of contempt pass over his shadowed expression as he registered her defiance.

"I will show you how very wrong you are," The Railmaster hissed, unfurling his inhumanly long, black-clawed fingers. Before Alessandra could grab her weapon off the floor to defend herself, the Railmaster snatched the meat hook and threw it into the Soul Engine's open maw. "You'll not be needing that."

His prey now disarmed and vulnerable, the Railmaster tore into Alessandra's back with flesh-rending claws, his hands flagellating her skin like an ice-cold barbed whip. But over the course of this harrowing night, Alessandra had grown a tolerance for pain she never thought possible – on top of her already thick New Yorker skin – so she clenched her teeth and bore the Railmaster's assault. Focusing through her agony, Alessandra observed her enemy and soon realized that she felt the jagged edge of each claw, the wind whipped by each of the Railmaster's fingers – the shadow man had to become corporeal to attack her!

Fueled by his desire to punish Alessandra for her insubordination, his smoke form had become solid. The Railmaster was vulnerable.

"You will walk these rails as a Shade under my hand, devoid of life and hope, until the march of time grinds you to dust – that is your fate, special girl," The Railmaster cast down blow after blow, but he was too absorbed in his own platitudes to watch as Alessandra's bandaged hand reached for the steel tip of the meat hook that still protruded a few inches out of the Soul Engine. The otherworldly heat of the phantom fire had emblazoned the hook with a searing white glow, like a poker left to smolder in the heart of a fireplace.

"You're wrong… about me… about us…," Even as the Railmaster gored her back and she heard the sizzle of her palm skin burning as she wrapped her hand around the superheated hook, Alessandra felt a surge of power course through her. "Deep down you're scared of the living because you know how this ends. We beat your goddamn labyrinth, killed your lackies, and now I'm here for you. You just can't face the truth… that my brother beat you! That I BEAT YOU!"

With an emboldened swing that would've impressed the viking warriors of old, Alessandra spun around and brought the shimmering white tip of the meat hook down onto the peak of the Railmaster's head, piercing his phantasmic skull and silencing the conductor as whatever life inside him suddenly shuddered to a halt! The Railmaster fell to his knees, an incomprehensible murmuring escaping his mouthless lips as the hook blazed with soul fire, sizzling away the whips of smoke that composed the once-mighty wraith. To finish the job — and add a little extra insult to injury — Alessandra yanked the hook forward, tearing the smoldering metal through the Railmaster's face before his body hit the floor and exploded across the compartment in a pathetic dusting of silver sand.

With the Railmaster dispatched, the adrenaline in Alessandra's veins slowed and she began to experience the excruciating pain that her body had ignored during those few precious moments of survival. Her back was bloodied with a cacophony of lash marks that stained her flayed shirt a deep crimson and her right hand, already mangled and crooked from the Swine's surprise attack, was now blackened, its skin made brittle like charred tree bark by the Soul Engine's supernatural fire. Alessandra knew that she would likely lose her right hand after the events of this grueling night, but at this point, that loss barely registered in the steel cage of her mind — if it meant her survival, it was a price she was willing to pay. She took one more deep breath, her slashed back and bruised lungs screaming with each inhale, but Alessandra knew her ordeal wasn't finished yet.

Limping to the sides of the Soul Engine, the wounded waitress began to open every valve and unscrew every lock and safety measure she could find. She didn't know anything about engines, but with the sabotage she had in mind, that ignorance was probably a strength. As she mangled its mechanical veins, the Soul Engine began to shudder and roar, rocking back and forth, threatening to break free of its metal housing as the souls inside erupted into an uncontrollable blaze, spitting white fireballs from the engine's mouth as cracks fissured across its black pipes.

Meltdown was imminent, but Alessandra still took a moment to rest her crippled hand atop the Soul Engine and whisper a final prayer for Bruno as the spirits trapped inside were finally freed.

With her brother avenged and the Nocturne Express barreling towards an early grave, Alessandra knew it was time to disembark. Struggling her way through the final set of doors, she entered the train's cockpit, a cramped little space normally meant for a single MTA worker to pilot the subway trains from stop to stop. However, though this compartment seemed the most modern of the last couple train cars she had fought through, Alessandra saw that the driver was anything but ordinary metro transit fare.

The only other soul with her in the cockpit was a vacant faced Shade, his body fused into the very train itself as if he was a ghost who had become corporeal halfway through phasing through the sheet metal wall. Wires and diodes were burrowed into the gray skin of his outspread arms like he had been crucified at the heart of some demonic motherboard, his nervous system as a nexus point for the train's twisted operating systems. The driver's pupilless eyes showed no recognition as Alessandra entered the compartment.

As Alessandra turned her eyes from the unfortunate undead, she gazed through the front window – with the Nocturne Express' supernatural veil lifted, saw earthly light and landmarks she recognized! At the far end of the tunnel, Alessandra saw the glow of lights from an oncoming train platform, and soon spotted a sign embossed into the tile wall denoting it as part of New York's iconic Grand Central Station. Something in her gut told her that this was the last stop before the End of the Line that Bruno had warned her about.

"Shit…" Alessandra murmured as she looked over the menagerie of cockpit controls and levers, at a loss for where to begin when it came to piloting this barreling bullet. But just as doubt began to seep into the panic at the edges of her mind, a mutilated, modulated voice spoke in her ear:

"Is he dead…?" the driver asked in a voice like an old dial-up modem being dragged through an arid desert. "The Railmaster… is he…?"

"Yes," Alessandra assured the driver, his pupils never rolling forward from the inside of his skull. "I killed him. He's gone."

"I can feel his grip… loosen," the driver gasped with a grating mechanical moan. "I am free… and you… must get off this train."

"Can you help me do that?" Alessandra asked, hope renewed as she watched Grand Central rocket ever closer, her window of escape near to closing. "I can try to get you out of these wires —"

"No," the driver spoke with all the force his modulated voice could muster, surprising Alessandra with this sudden burst of life. "I will not survive…if taken offline… but I can free you…" Though she knew the driver could not see her, Alessandra gave a grateful nod, stern as she processed this Shade's sacrifice.

"I cannot stop the Nocturne in the waking world… but I can slow it down enough for you to… disembark," the driver instructed. As Alessandra moved towards the cabin door, the cockpit controls began to move on under the driver's psychic control, warning lights flashing as the platform neared. Feeling the blistering wind against her singed and scarred face, Alessandra bent her knees and steeled herself for one last tribulation.

"Now!" the driver cried, his voice glitching into a robotic wail as the Nocturne slowed ever so slightly, just long enough for Alessandra to leap from the side of the barreling train!

Tucking her head and her wounded arm into her chest and curling herself into as tight of a ball as she could muster, Alessandra crashed into the hard concrete platform, her cannonball journey stopping only when she collided with one of the thick steel support beams lining the platform's edge. She was bruised and battered, her skin scored with stripped flesh and friction burns, a handful of her ribs were smashed to pieces, and her right hand was all but useless, but as Alessandra was swarmed by a concerned crowd of early morning commuters, she knew that she was alive and finally free.

As she was loaded onto a paramedic's stretcher, Alessandra cast one last glance down the dark tunnel, towards that fabled End of the Line. She watched a ghostly white light erupt at the tunnel's end, followed by a chorus of phantasmagoric wails as, somewhere in the bowels of the Earth, the Soul Engine exploded and the Nocturne Express finally derailed. But all the other commuters went about their day, never registering the supernatural shockwave – unlike Alessandra, the veil of the beyond was still pulled snuggly over their mortal eyes. They were lucky.

As she was carried towards an ambulance that waited outside the glinting brass-crowned doors of Grand Central Station, Alessandra didn't know what lay ahead for her – she had no idea how long it would take to recover, how she would explain Bruno's fate to her parents, or how she would make peace with the many nightmares she had beheld that night.

But for the moment, she was content to simply reemerge out onto the bustling streets of New York City and bask in the gray morning light once more.

YELLOW KING,
SILVER SCREEN

IN THE SUMMER OF 1943, it seemed like all of America had come to a standstill as the country watched with bated breath as GI's sailed across the great Atlantic to battle fascism on its home turf. But there was another battle raging back on American shores – a battle of morale. Gas vouchers, victory gardens, and scrap metal drives had become the everyday realities for those left behind – busywork to keep the grim reality of the Second World War at the back of their minds.

It was in a little town called Hollywood that the great commanders of this war of distraction called the shots. It was the solemn, self-important duty of those masters like Louie B. Mayer and David O. Selznick to keep the public entertained and at ease, at least as best as they could manage. Even as the world was engulfed in conflict, the film reels continued to roll - the show must go on, after all.

Desperate to keep up with audiences' demands for escapism, 1943 saw studios release more films than any year before it, exporting them from the arid California desert out to the screens of the world as their humble tribute to the war effort. However, it wasn't only the big players that were fighting for their spot on the Silver Screen – this was the opportunity that Hollywood's little guys had been waiting for to launch their creative dreams like the Warners and Paramounts before them.

One of these little studios was the yet-undiscovered Magnificent Pictures, run out of a carpet-warehouse-turned-soundstage in Riverside and bankrolled on the dime of railway mogul Peter Faulke, whose son, William, just happened to be the President of the upstart studio.

To the elder Faulke, this studio was merely another passing fad that his son would obsess over for a year or two at most before throwing the whole thing away like a Christmas toy that had lost its luster by February – however, the cinematic bug had thoroughly bitten young William and by 1943, he had it in his head that he was meant to become a capital G "Great Artist." But how many other dreamers had made such a claim before him, and how many would make that same boast in the decades to come? Hollywood has a way of directing its own story, plans and plots be damned – and William Faulke was destined to learn that fact firsthand.

But as is the case with all good films, this story began with a script.

Knowing that his youth and inexperience would give him little bargaining power when going up against the Big Studios, William turned to the only other resource at his disposal that had a chance at evening the playing field: his father's vast wealth. Using the Faulke family fortune, William was able to buy the best equipment, bring on the best cinematographers and producers from across the country, and even poach some of the day's biggest stars away from the studios that had made them famous, all just by waving the right size check under their noses. The only thing money couldn't buy in the film industry was taste, but no one was about to tell William that.

This spending spree brought William into contact with eccentric and illustrious screenwriter Charlie Thurston – once a powerhouse of Hollywood's grandiose swords-and-sandals epics, Charlie's heyday had come and gone by the time he met Faulke. At that point, no one in the industry had seen Charlie out in public for a year and a half, and the few that did manage to catch him on the telephone for a rare minute or two reported back that old Chuck was working on something new, something big… but he maintained that the viewing public wasn't ready for whatever revolution in storytelling he had devised.

When William heard about this mystery screenwriter, he spared no expense trying to woo Charlie into lending his new script to Magnificent to be their debut picture. After months of letters, phone calls, private investigators, and bribes that were rumored to include an all-gold Mercedes, William finally secured an audience with Mr. Thurston in his secluded Beverly Hills bungalow. No one knows what they talked about behind Thurston's cedarwood door, but William would tell stories of the encounter in the years to come, claiming that Charlie had looked like a man possessed, his office cluttered with torn script pages and mountains of empty coffee cups stacked around his typewriter like some shrine. Apparently, what sealed the deal for Charlie was William's insistence that the film would be shot in color, even though the process was incredibly expensive and most films of the era were still shot in classic black and white. William had been enamored with Technicolor after its dazzling debut in *The Wizard of Oz* four years earlier and would spare no expense to replicate that rainbow spectacle in his own film.

"Color is essential to this story," Charlie had explained to William, a frenetic energy possessing the writer as he held his script pages in a passionate grip. "The Yellow King must be seen in his full glory."

William couldn't agree more, so he purchased the exclusive rights to Charlie's 'masterpiece', *The Court of the Yellow King*, for a princely sum. However, even though Thurston had been paid a small fortune for his work, the eclectic writer would be dead only weeks later, found by his housekeeper hanging by the neck from his bungalow's creaking ceiling fan.

Some said that he committed suicide after someone in the industry threatened to out him as a homosexual – it was a well-known but unspoken secret that Charlie Thurston had enjoyed his share of dalliances with a few pool boys and strapping hotel bellhops; Others claimed he had gotten in deep with the wrong people on the wrong side of town and paid the price – by the 40s, the East Coast mafia families had moved West and gangsters were snug in bed with many of Hollywood's top brass; Some gossips even put the blame on the estranged family that Charlie had only mentioned on a handful of occasions, speaking about them to close friends in the hushed, fearful voice of a child crouching beneath a table to hide from daddy's wrath. No matter the reason, Charlie Thurston was laid to rest in Forest Lawn Cemetery, and even Bogart made an appearance at the funeral to see the writer off to the big studio lot in the sky.

However, William Faulke did little mourning on the behalf of poor Chuck Thurston – he had got what he came for, and now that Charlie was dead, his final script was sure to earn William and Magnificent a slew of posthumous accolades when the film premiered.

As the pre-production process for *The Court of the Yellow King* moved into high gear, William became obsessed with overseeing all elements of the production personally, handpicking everyone from the director to the set builders to the PAs, his need for control evolving so far that he refused to let any other eyes look upon Thurston's script besides his own.

The film's director, Jacob Maldinano, claimed that "Will would never let me read a page of the script, even as our first day of shooting loomed. When I asked him how the hell I was supposed to direct some movie I didn't know the story to, he just said 'Figure it out – that's what the money's for.' I guess he was right. A payday is a payday, so we just grinned and bared it as long as the checks cleared."

The arduous production hobbled along this way for months, with William verbally dictating any and all elements of the script that needed to be funneled down to his artisans. By the time August arrived, the Magnificent soundstage was filled with colossal sets of opulent castle halls and dark, foreboding crypts and hundreds of stage swords and prop spears lined the storage rooms in anticipation for some grand battle scene yet to be filmed. However, the production ground to a halt when the overworked costume designer, Georgina Hastings, suddenly quit the project, protesting her treatment at William's hand.

The night before her sudden exit, William had stormed into Georgina's studio, demanding to see what she had come up with for the Yellow King's robes. By this point, William had vetoed over a dozen different designs, furious that she was not giving the King "the grandeur he deserved", all while never allowing Georgina to reference the script herself.

When Georgina showed him her most recent attempt, he flew into a rage, tearing her studio apart and burning the silken robes with a cigarette lighter. Georgina had worked for demanding producers before and had cut her teeth costuming massive productions like *Gone with The Wind*, but after Faulke's late night raid, she finally reached her breaking point under the thumb of this tyrannical trust fund child.

Georgina's exit left the production in a lurch – they were only days away from shooting and they didn't have a single garment for their eponymous Yellow King. Seeing that William was distraught and growing more unhinged by the day, director Jacob Maldinano eventually convinced the fraying young Faulke to allow him to reach out to a designer friend of his that he was certain could do William's vision justice. However, Maldinano made William agree to one condition before he would make the call – he had to let this designer see the script. With the entire production on the line, it was the only way. Pale and murmuring, William finally agreed, sending a copy of the script by private courier to the Malibu home of one Lucius D'Couture.

Lucius was something of a phenom in the arena of early 20th century fashion, seizing the attention of the world with their daring eye for the abstract, both through their designs and their unorthodox personal life. Making their debut on the runways and in social clubs of Paris back in the early 30s, Lucius had gone on to craft gowns worn by Gretta Garbo on the red carpet to fashion-forward pantsuits for Billie Holiday to evening wear for then-princess Elizabeth II of England. But don't be fooled – Lucius was just as unique as their fantastic fabric creations.

Once they made the move from Paris to California, it was common for one to see Lucius drinking martinis in reserved booths at Los Angeles' finest clubs, pontificating about the obtuse nature of existence, all while wearing a faceful of expressionistic vaudevillian makeup and an explosive outfit that combined the masculinity of a tuxedo with the demur feminin-ity of a ball gown – always original garments of D'Couture's own creation, of course.

"Gender is like chiffon, my dear," Lucius would coo to curious cock-tail companions when asked about their androgynous attitude. "You can try to flatten it all you like, but you'll never truly be rid of the wrinkles. And why would you want to be?"

Despite – or perhaps because of – their flamboyance, Lucius D'Cou-ture established themself as the delirious Dionysus of the Los Angeles art scene, in large part because of the intoxicating self-confidence they exuded, even when sharing the same ballroom as well-known showbiz conserva-tives like W.C. Fields. It was this mastery over their craft and their convic-tions that convinced Jacob Maldinano that Lucius was the only person in Hollywood that could bring the Yellow King to life in just a matter of days. Thrilled by the challenge, Lucius agreed to take on this Herculean task if only for the sheer desire to prove that it could be done.

On a steamy August night, Lucius sat in a red leather armchair, listening to the waves crash against the Malibu shoreline as they read over the script for *The Court of The Yellow King*, titillated by the idea that they were only one of three pairs of eyes that had ever read these coveted words. As they swirled a stalk of celery against the frothing rim of their third Bloody Mary, Lucius read about an ornate golden hall, filled with robed, faceless servants surrounding a throne of black diamond; about a great keep that scraped the stars, dwarfing the biblical Tower of Babylon; and about a great and terrible ruler, shrouded in a veil of unending night, his fingers reaching out across his shadowed kingdom in search of some mysterious, existential purpose known only to Charlie Thurston and the Yellow King himself.

The script itself was a narrative mess, filled with scenes of unfilmable visions and grand cosmic designs that would surely go over the heads of any run-of-the-mill audience or stuffy film executive – but that's exactly what Lucius liked about it. Lucius was already seen as 'unfathomable' by the outside world, so who better to breathe life into this impossible golden monarch? With only a precious few days before the designs were due, Lucius took their phone off the hook, readied their easel, and set out to seek an audience with the King.

Adhering strictly to the process that had already brought them success, Lucius first went about bringing their subject to life in oil paint on a tall, narrow canvas not dissimilar in size to a standing mirror. Lucius would claim that they were not in control of themself during these painting sessions – they merely closed their eyes and "let the spirits of those mythical muses from ancient times inhabit my hand and guide me to my destiny." Lucius believed the brush strokes gave them a blueprint to the flow of their fabrics and gave them mastery over the abstract forms that they would soon usher into reality – "like the automatic writing that psychics and spiritualists use to communicate with the dead," D'Couture would explain with a twinkle in corner of their jade eyes, "except my conjuring is the real deal."

As their brush strokes flew over the canvas with the self-assured vision of an oracle, a cryptic figure began to take shape on Lucius' canvas: It was slender, almost inhumanly tall, draped in a hooded golden robe adorned with fiery orange accents that made the shawl seem as if its fibers were woven out of cresting sunset. The garment's flowing sleeves mimicked the form of a Japanese kimono, while the black banner that cascaded down over its narrow shoulders was inspired by an Orthodox priest's holy stole – though even Lucius couldn't imagine to what deity this cosmic clergyman might pray.

Atop its hooded head, Lucius painted an iron crown with long points that crept up towards the heavens, and D'Couture further designed a resplendent aureole that fanned out from the being's back like the gold-leafed halos found in the holy art of the ancient Byzantines. Next, Lucius' brush moved down to the being's face as they adorned it with a mouthless iron mask, accentuated with silver tears running from its round, unblinking eyes down the mask's expressionistic cheekbones. A lesser artist would have hesitated to create a costume that explicitly masks and blinds the actor wearing it, but Lucius knew that to achieve the untethered esoteric madness that permeated every page of Thurston's script they would have to strip the Yellow King of any humanity, in favor of an otherworldly aesthetic.

However, as Lucius' painting progressed, their artistic fugue state began to take a greater hold over the fashion designer's soul. As each brush stroke dug into the canvas with a mounting electricity, compelled by something beyond their understanding ... truly, some other force was piloting Lucius' hand now, but it felt different than the 'muses' D'Couture had so flippantly described. Soon, Lucius closed their eyes as their power of sight was rendered pointless by this artistic possession, until – at the euphoric climax of Lucius' frenetic state – their paintbrush snapped like a twig between their fingers!

Lurched out of their dreamlike state, Lucius opened their eyes just in time to catch a glimpse of something moving behind them in the reflection of their window! A quick flash of movement, a tail of yellow fabric billowing out from behind the armchair, then suddenly – *CRASH!* – Lucius' half-finished bloody mary smashed against the floor, sending glass shards and tomato puree chunks splashing across the studio, seeping into the hardwood floor like the blood of some felled beast.

"Damn it all!" Lucius growled as they spun around on their heels, their creative trance now thoroughly interrupted. D'Couture had a very strict rule in their studio – they were never to be disturbed while they were working, even if the matter was life of death. For Lucius, the art always came first – but it seemed this intruder did not share their commitment.

"Leave me be, you jackals!" Lucius demanded as they snatched a gleaming pallet knife from their easel and began to patrol their home for the source of this disturbance. It was probably another paparazzi ghoul, slinking around in the hopes of catching Lucius in some compromising imbroglio. However, after fruitless minutes of searching, Lucius found the house was silent as a tomb, the front door still locked tight. No one had come in or out during Lucius' painting session, and the designer didn't even have a cat to blame for the unexplained mischief.

After their rage deflated into a weary befuddlement, Lucius returned to the canvas, assuring themself that the fallen glass had been the result of some minor earthquake, one of the many imperceptible tremors that shook the Californian coast from time to time – though that did little to explain what had possessed the artist with enough vigor to suddenly snap their paintbrush in two. D'Couture was a passionate person, but not a violent one.

As Lucius stared at the golden robbed being on the canvas in front of them, they realized that there was still something missing... something they couldn't quite put their finger on... but the faceless whisper that had guided their creation until moments ago had gone silent for now. With their zen shattered, Lucius took this as a sign from the universe to pour another drink and wait for fresh inspiration to strike.

It was out on their balcony that inspiration struck Lucius as they sipped from a glass of scotch and gazed out on the black waters of the Pacific. An unseasonable fog had rolled in from the deep ocean, blanketing the rocky shores of Malibu in a dreamy night haze. From the depths of the gray mists, Lucius watched a verdant green light fade into view, shimmering like the beacon of some emerald lighthouse, floating alone in the heart of the dark surf. Whether it was the lights of some bobbing ship or a reflection from some beachside settlement, Lucius didn't care – inspiration had struck and D'Couture returned to their easel.

Soon, an ornate lantern began to take shape on the canvas, clutched piously in the robed being's outstretched hand like a ceremonial censer swung back and forth at Catholic mass. Except there was no holy incense behind this lantern's black iron frame and distorted sea glass panes, but instead there burned a glowing green flame, flickering with a supernatural allure. A sacred relic fit for a ruler as enchanting and enigmatic as the Yellow King.

It wasn't until Lucius completed the final brush strokes on the sanctified lantern that they emerged from their tunnel vision and realized that the green light had disappeared from its foggy resting place in the dark waters below. For a moment, the seaside night was pregnant with an uneasy silence… until the glow suddenly erupted like starfire inside Lucius' studio, bathing the stunned D'Couture in an unearthly jade light!

The glow seemed to distort the very space around Lucius, warping the air around them like a liquid funhouse gallery. But before the fashion designer could search for the source of this disarming miasma of color and sensation, a thunderous voice echoed from the empty air behind the canvas:

"Who are you to seek an audience with the Yellow King?" the voice boomed like a cascade of rolling thunder as the green light coalesced into a radiant orb in front of D'Couture's painting. It floated like a tantalizing will o' wisp, pulsing with the rhythm of some palpitating organ – horrifying as the vision was, Lucius felt the light call to them, beckoning…

"Who calls forth to summon the Lord of the Deepest Reaches, the Great Deacon of the Umbral Expanse?" the powerful voice demanded again, now seeming to reverberate from inside the confines of Lucius' own skull.

"I-I am Lucius D'Couture," Lucius called back, struggling to maintain the composure in their voice as a low hypnotic hum emanated from the green beacon. An ordinary person would have been reduced to abject fear where they stood, but Lucius prided themselves on being anything but ordinary. "I seek – I demand an audience with the Yellow King."

For a moment, there was only silence and the green glow. Had Lucius' boldness staggered even this supernatural force? But just as movement began to return to Lucius' limbs, just as they thought to reach towards the floating orb, the canvas in front of them began to move.

But it didn't shake or jump or fly across the room – the face of the painting, which had been nothing but solid canvas fibers just moments ago, began to ripple like gentle waves across a tranquil puddle. Emerging from the liquid cloth, a scarlet gloved hand reached out from some unknowable depth in the heart of the rippling painting. An inky black mana spread from its pores as its slender fingers reached for the green light, the swirling black- ness condensed around the source of the emerald glow. The dark energy twisted and reassembled itself until finally taking the shape of the lantern from Lucius' painting, its ornate handle clutched in the scarlet claws.

"You demand nothing. He is as old as the First Starlight and as unyielding as the Grave of All Time. No mortal eyes may look upon the Yellow King, lest they devolve into madness."

Now seemingly strengthened by its tether to this mortal plane, the voice's master decided to make its grand entrance. Slipping out of the painting as easily as one would emerge from a bath, a figure clad in a blind- eyed, silver-teared mask and a golden robe of woven sunset stood in front of Lucius, holding the green flame lantern aloft like Carrion, the boatman of the River Styx. "I am but the Emissary of Our Golden Master… and you are his prophet."

"Prophet?" Lucius echoed, their voice a mix of astoundment and confusion – despite the otherworldly vision before them, there was still a spark of honor that came with such a title. They had to know more. "Why me? What is it I'm supposed to be prophesying?"

"You may call yourself an artist," the Emissary declared, "But you are a rare being, one of the holy chosen touched by a cosmic inspiration, all in the service of our lord, the Crowned Devourer. It is your destiny to usher his arrival into this realm so that he may claim it as another addition to his empire of vast night."

"The writer…," Lucius realized, mind fumbling back through their memory of the script. It had not been some mere stage play – it was a gospel. "Charlie Thurston! Was he one? Was he a prophet?"

"Yes," the Emissary spoke, its mouth never visible beneath its unblinking mask. "The storysmith performed his duty, birthed our Master's texts into this realm. Then he ascended."

"Ascended where?" Lucius asked, hesitation in their voice as the Emissary floated around them, its robes gliding across the studio floor like a slinking golden river.

"To somewhere greater," the lipless voice whispered in Lucius' ear, it's very shadow seeming to lay on D'Couture in a dark embrace. "Do you not wish to evolve? This world does not wish to understand you, your genius. Those others are but specks in the vacuous maw of Existence – but if you offer yourself to the arms of the King in Yellow, our Master will raise you up to his kingdom, to stand by his side in the Endless Unknown. Do you wish to become greater, Lucius D'Couture?"

As Lucius stared ahead, imagining these great unknowable worlds in realms beyond, they felt a sort of comfort wash over them and a glamor begin to tint the edges of their eyes. Finally, a place where they would be understood, a place where they would be appreciated for who they were – where they wouldn't be looked upon like some malady. Finally, after all this time, evolution was within Lucius' reach.

"Yes."

"Good," the Emissary groaned with a perceptible mirth – if it had a mouth, one could've sworn the being was smiling. "You are blessed with the cosmic mandate to create the great helm of our lord and to grant him passage to this world."

Before Lucius had a chance to shake off his dazzlement and ask how exactly he was meant to build such a helm, the Emissary reached its robed arm out in front of D'Couture, opening its palm and spreading its digits disjointedly wide. With a flex of the being's fingers, every piece of gold in Lucius' house – their jewelry, tableware, award statues – flew across the room at impossible speeds until they abruptly stopped, floating mere feet away from Lucius' face. As the Emissary closed its fist, the metals began to boil in midair, pieces melding into one another until an orb of molten gold hovered in front of the designer, reflecting Lucius' face in its warping, shimmering surface. The Emissary did not seem to cast a reflection.

"Go ahead," The Emissary coaxed Lucius, seeming to take a cruel satisfaction in the spectacle. "Touch it."

Lucius was hesitant as they reached out towards the ball of steaming metal, feeling the intense heat radiating from its beautiful surface. However, just as Lucius' fingers grazed the molten golden, they found that it was as cool as clay, even pleasant to the touch! Like a child on the eve of some new discovery, Lucius dug their fingers deeper into the gold, letting the shimmering metal droplets cascade down their forearms and stain their skin a regal yellow.

"This is incredible..." Lucius murmured, more to themself than to any other presence in the room. The Emissary silently retreated from the designer's side as inspiration began to take hold of D'Couture. Lucius began to sculpt the gold in midair, their movements punctuated with frantic finger strokes and excited breaths, their eyes as wide as if they were hopped up on every speed pill and popper in the state of California. This was the cosmic inspiration that the Emissary had spoken of, and Lucius was fully in the grip of its rapture.

Soon, features began to form in the crude gold – the spires of a twisted crown, a hundred eyes sculpted into the face of a mask as mouthless as the Emissary's own, but far grander in its filigree and adornments. Tapering down from the golden helm, Lucius carefully molded an ornate gorget collar to lay atop the King's neck and shoulders, its edges decorated with sculptures of coiled creatures that were beyond alien, unlike any Earthly species. By the time Lucius finished and stood, gold-stained and fanatical, in front of their creation, the great helm looked like a ceremonial headpiece fit for the tomb of Charlemagne or as a death mask for the Pharaohs of old.

"Your holy purpose is complete, prophet," The Emissary congratulated Lucius as it glided over gracefully as a phantom and examined the helm. "You have earned your audience. Are you prepared to meet the King in Yellow, the Final Ruler of the Unsleeping Realms?"

"Yes, God! I'm ready," Lucius begged, tears cutting swaths through mascara as they streamed down their face. So powerful was D'Couture's desperation to ascend that they fell to their knees, bathed in the vertigo glow of the Emissary's green flame. "Make me more than I am! Take me away from here!"

"First, you must swear fealty," The Emissary commanded as it held the lantern up to Lucius' face, as if the fashion designer was meant to pray their allegiance to the very flame itself. "Pledge your unending loyalty to the King Beyond the Golden Veil."

"I swear!" Lucius wept, so possessed by revelation that they grabbed the lantern with buckled fingers and kissed the glass as if paying tribute to a pope or penitence to a divine lover.

"Then prepare for His Majesty's arrival," The Emissary declared as the lantern light began to shine with greater intensity, its mesmerizing green hue turning a pure starlight white. A sea of echoing voices began to call out from the light, speaking in tongues no terrestrial ears had ever heard before, some sounding like songs, others like screams.

"It's beautiful…" was all the smiling Lucius had time to mutter before the white light erupted with an unearthly power, bathing the entire house in a blinding starlight! The white light was impossibly hot, scorching everything it touched – but Lucius D'Couture was still smiling as the lantern light turned their skin to insignificant dust, stripping the fashion designer's body down to the blackened bone.

The white light erupting forth like the pulses of a supernova, The Emissary recited a deep, alien chant as it lowered the great golden helm over Lucius' bare skull, anointing the charred skeleton with the great purpose that the cosmic priest had promised to bestow. An otherworldly glow shone from the helm's many eyes as a majestic robe stitched itself together from the blinding light itself, until it cradled the exalted bones in its gentle golden embrace.

The King in Yellow had claimed his new host.

When the Malibu Fire Department arrived in the early hours of the following morning, there wasn't much left of the D'Couture Estate to survey. The designer's home had been reduced to a burning pile of rubble, an unsightly black cigar tip smoldering on the pristine Pacific shoreline. All that remained unburnt was a blank white canvas, left untouched in the middle of what had once been the eccentric artist's studio.

Most folks just assumed there had been a gas leak – a pipe knocked loose by some small, unmemorable earthquake – an easy enough explanation for the destruction of a California house on an unstable cliffside. Some neighbors gossiped and said that the whole thing was some insurance scam or that Lucius had faked their own death to skip town and was now off living it up in Acapulco. The later theory wasn't as far off as one would think – after all, Lucius D'Couture did skip town, but where he went remains a mystery.

A few fire marshals suspected foul play after finding two sets of footprints in the ash heap, leading away from the remains of the house towards the cliffside before seeming to vanish off the edge. However, the D.A.

wasn't very keen on devoting resources to an investigation into "notorious fruit" Lucius D'Couture, so the incident was swiftly declared an accidental death and what little evidence there was ended up at the bottom of the County Sheriff's filing cabinet.

As for *The Court of the Yellow King*, the production was delayed again and again until Peter Faulke finally pulled the plug on his son's floundering studio. William was never the same and he never seemed to shake whatever passion had possessed him during his one and only film production. Plagued by the fact that he was never destined to be a prophet of any kind, William drank himself to death in the Sahara Casino in Las Vegas only four years later.

William's death shattered his notoriously stonefaced father, leading Peter to sell off most of his son's assets – including the bulk sale of all Magnificent Pictures property to Paramount in 1948. Though the *Court of the Yellow King* was shelved over 70 years ago, Charlie Thurston's script remains locked away somewhere in the Paramount vault, hidden in the shadows, gathering dust, biding its time until it can finally share its prophesies with the world.

How would you like an audience with the Yellow King, up on the silver screen? Coming next summer, or the summer after that, or the summer after that – he doesn't mind waiting until the time is right for his message. His premiere will come soon enough, on a red carpet made from starlight and malice. After all, what's a few more years in comparison to the infinite lifespan of an ageless one? Who knows, maybe he can even make you a star.

All it will cost is the price of admission, a few bucks for popcorn... and your mortal soul.

MARROW MUSIC

ARTEM OTCHENASH walked the banks of the Dnieper River, as he had
every morning for the last year. Retirement didn't suit him – all that nothingness that now filled his days. He was used to being productive, making
a contribution to the State like everyone else. Today, a particularly chilly
breeze blew off the lapping river waters, awakening the ache in Artem's
bad knee as the gust whistled its way through the streets of Kiev. The year
was 1987, and though the crimson banner and Soviet stars still flew above
the Ukrainian houses of government and bustling city squares, a feeling
of inevitable change was being whispered on the wind.

As Artem hiked his tweed jacket collar up around his leathery neck
and began his climb up Volodymyrska Hill towards the holy golden spires
of St. Michael's Monastery, he thought of the many cracks that were spider-
webbing their way across the facade of the USSR – *Glasnost* was opening
the Iron Curtain to the world for the first time in decades, rumors were
swirling concerning Boris Yeltin's resignation, Latvian schoolchildren were
calling for independence… Gorbachev couldn't hold this circus together
much longer. Even Artem could see that.

As the old Ukrainian reached the peak of Volodymyrska and stood
panting under the gaze of Saint Vladimir the Great, his mind traveled to
Gorbachev's recent release of political prisoners from the "Siberian reha-

bilitation camps" – not since Stalin's death had so many been freed from the gulags.

Though they hadn't been referred to as 'gulags' for decades, every Soviet citizen was well-accustomed to the looming threat of backbreaking, soul-crushing labor that awaited any dissidents who spoke out against the Party, no matter what name Khrushchev or Brezhnev or Gorbachev chose for them.

Artem knew these harsh realities better than most – he had been a small cog in the great machine of Soviet Silence, serving many years in the NKVD – the Soviet secret police.

You see, Artem had been only a boy of fifteen in 1941 when the Germans marched into Kiev. He had watched as the men in their sharp black uniforms arrested every Jew, socialist, Romani, and proud Ukrainian Nationalist they could find – some they rounded up under the guise of resettlement elsewhere in the Reich's growing empire, others they shot dead in the open street like one would cull a sick dog. In those days, information was scarce, but years later, Artem learned that 33,000 had been killed in just the first two days of the occupation, with another 150,000 to follow before the war's end, all thrown like broken marionettes into the Babi Yar ravine outside of the city.

Young Artem had wanted to fight back, to strike out at the Nazi occupiers with bottle rockets and his father's old hunting rifle, but his mother had stopped him, knowing that he would just become another corpse on the pile if he dared step out of line.

But two years later in 1943, Artem was a man of eighteen when he watched the thunderous boots of the Red Army retake the city, crushing German Panzer tanks as easily as if they were tin cans left abandoned by the roadside. Of course, a peasant boy like Artem Otchenash was too young to remember when Stalin's Purge had wiped out the migrants and *intelligentsia* of Kiev ten years before, just as the Nazis had done in '41 – all

he knew was that these were the Soviet Supermen that Stalin had promised, and Artem wanted to be just like them.

As Kiev pulled herself from the rubble of the Second World War,
the idealistic boy submitted his application to serve as part of the Militsiya,
the standard police force of the USSR – but due to his high marks on his
physical exams and his steadfast belief in the absolute good of the Commu-
nist Party, Artem was instead selected for the elite ranks of the NKVD.
He was told that he would be the first line of defense on the Soviet home
front against instigators, terrorists, and undesirables who sought to sabotage the peace that his countrymen had so heroically spilled their blood to
achieve – and for a long time, Artem believed he was serving a noble cause.
But as Corinthians says, one day we all must put away childish things and
see the world for what it is.

Artem did his best to put those old ghosts out of his mind as he
strolled towards the market at Bessarabska Square, another important
element of his morning ritual. As he perused the bruised apples and spud-
eyed potatoes that lined the market stalls, he soon came to a small table
lined with boxes of junkyard finds and dog-eared records. Standing behind
the table was the booth's stout proprietor, a frog-eyed little man known to
the locals as simply "Nuck".

Nuck was a connoisseur of the lost and the broken, a preserver of
forgotten history – he might not look it, but back in the day, such a man
would've been considered a legitimate danger to the Party. Back in the old
days, men like Artem would've been sent after men like Nuck, but with
restrictions on media and Western imports loosening under Gorbechov's
watch, the portly salesman was able to peddle his wares in relative peace.

"Ey *Malish*, good to see you," Nuck greeted Artem as he slowly
approached his table. Even though Nuck was only a few years Artem's
elder, he still chose to use a child's nickname whenever two met, much to
Artem's aggravation.

"Hello, you old *razvaluha*," Artem returned the greeting in kind, complete with a pearl of slang that equated Nuck to a busted-down car. "Any good finds today?"

"Ah, not too much – this week's been a slow one," Nuck complained, throwing his gnarled palms up in the air as if tossing the blame up to God. "But I did find a few crates of records being tossed to the curb by some old widow. Take a look, see what catches your fancy."

Artem nodded and began to thumb his way through the crate of record sleeves – he wasn't much of a musical man himself, but sometimes treasures lurked amongst Nuck's scraps. Many of the covers bore the red star logo of Melodiya, the state-owned record label. Classical symphonies of Tchaikovsky and Shostakovich dominated Nuck's collection, alongside a few recordings of famed Soviet mezzo-soprano Alla Pugacheva and the short-lived Russian rock band Kruiz… but Artem's blood ran cold as he came across a labeless record, wrapped in a sleeve of crumpled brown paper, marked with a single name: *Sergei Kiselyov.*

"Where did you find this?" Artem asked, his tongue suddenly dry, his voice hoarse.

"In the box, along with the others! I don't know," Nuck shrugged, disinterestedly tinkering with a broken-down clock. "Why, you want it?"

By the time Nuck turned back around, Artem was already gone, the hand-packaged record under his arm and a handful of coins strewn haphazardly across Nuck's table as payment.

Artem could barely catch his breath as he made a hasty retreat back to his apartment – every time he tried to breathe, every time he glanced at the name on the record sleeve, it felt like his chest was being crushed tighter and tighter around his struggling lungs. His fingers quaked as he fumbled to unlock the front door to his apartment building, the copper keys threatening to fall from his quivering fingers to the curb at any moment. When the deadlock finally clicked open, Artem stormed through the lobby, ignoring his usual morning greeting from his elderly neighbor, Mrs. Ponomarenko, as he flew up the stairs with a frantic speed faster than his rusty joints had moved in years. In her knitting circle days later, Ponomarenko would go on to describe Artem as a man possessed, looking over his shoulder every few seconds as if he expected to find a demon latched to his back. How right she was.

Artem burst into his apartment on the third floor, slamming the heavy wooden door behind him and locking every bolt and chain imaginable before finally stopping to suck down a lungful of air. Why was he acting like this? It was just a record, just a coincidence… Why did he suddenly feel this spectre of malice hanging over him? After all, Sergei Kiselyov was dead.

"Yes, Sergei Kiselyov is dead," Artem reminded himself over and over, attempting to drown out the creeping fears that clawed at the recesses of his brain with cold reason. "He's been dead for thirty years."

But try as he might, Artem's heart took little comfort from the reassurances ricocheting around his brain. He had known Sergei well, all those years ago – at one point in time, he would've dared to call them friends. Sergei had been one of the most accomplished violinists in all of the Balkans, classically trained by the Russian masters and infused with a God-given talent to move the hearts of those who listened to him. He wrote his first violin sonata at the tender age of seventeen, to commemorate the Bolsehvick revolution that led to Ukraine's annexation by the then-adolescent Soviet Union – many Communists played Sergei's sonata as a song of celebration, but Kiselyov had truly written the piece as a funeral dirge, to mourn the independent Ukraine that he watched crumble before his very eyes. That sonata would be the first of many subtle acts of defiance that Sergei would commit as artistic rebellion against the Soviet state.

After Artem's father passed away from pneumonia in the winter of '33, Artem and his mother were relocated to a different apartment building across the river from where they had once lived. Settling in was difficult and

Artem's mother spent most of her time at the cannery where she worked, so most days one could find the young Artem kicking a hard rubber ball around the apartment building lobby as he struggled to busy himself. It was on one of these gray afternoons that Artem first heard a soft melody wafting down the staircase from somewhere above, calling to him like a sweet siren song.

Following the melody like a trail of proverbial breadcrumbs, Artem found himself on the top floor of the apartment building, standing outside a door not unlike his own, from behind which the divine notes called to him. Without a second thought, Artem turned the knob and found the door to be unlocked, as if the song had itself been invitation enough to enter.

As the green door slowly swung open, Artem found himself face to face with the source of the enchanting music: standing in the center of the room, beneath a fogged glass skylight, was a slender man, dressed in a sage green lily-patterned robe and frayed slippers – even though the man was only in his thirties, regal streaks of ashen white peppered his hair at the temples. Many would've described his look as Bohemian, but to Artem, the slender man looked like a wizard from a story book, casting spells in his top-floor sanctum.

But what really drew Artem's attention was the beautiful cedarwood violin that was tucked into the crook of the man's shoulder – Artem would later learn that it was the last of its kind, an antique instrument constructed by a master craftsman in the little village Markneukirchen, Germany, made special for this musical magician. A sleek horsehair bow glided over the violin strings as smoothly as a waterbug dancing across a still pond, pulling ethereal chords from the soul of the instrument and giving them life in the air around the musician. It wasn't until the tune came to a haunting end and the last vibrations of sound echoed from the belly of the violin that the player turned his sunken stare to look upon his uninvited guest. That was the first time Artem saw Sergei Kiselyov's blue eyes – they were the color of the ice on the Dnieper River, and they pierced straight into the boy's very core.

The young Artem cowered, ready to slam the door shut and run back down the stairs as if he had just witnessed some great secret… but the boy stopped short as he watched the slender man's rosy lips curled up into a smile beneath his well-groomed beard.

"Would you like to hear another, *Malish?*"

So, Artem spent the rest of the day sitting on a canary yellow couch, sipping herbal tea and listening as Sergei played him song after song on his violin – some were classics, others pieces of Sergei's own devising, and others still were improvisations, the master musician plucking inspiration from out of the air as easily as one would pick an apple from a tree branch. When Artem's mother finally returned from work to collect her son, the night sky was dark but the violin still played. For the first time since Papa Otchenash's death, a spark of joy returned to the young boy's heart, all thanks to the mysterious musician with his endless songs.

Back in the present day, Artem didn't feel that joyous spark as he lowered himself into his creaky leather armchair, the record still sheathed in his hands. With a final, determined breath that only seemed to widen the black pit that was growing in his stomach, Artem gingerly pulled away the strips of tape that bound the record's paper wrappings, gently slipping the vinyl disc free from its confines to reveal… bones. Specifically, the bones of a hand, its fingers cracked and buckled in all the wrong directions. They were imprinted across the face of the record – or more accurately, the grooves of the record were printed into the very bones themselves.

Artem had seen a few of these before, back in his NKVD days, but they were illegal and therefore very rare – this record had been printed on an x-ray sheet. The street names for these kinds of homemade records were *bone music* or simply *ribs* – due to the shortage of vinyl in the USSR during 50s and 60s and the desire to spread contraband music under the radar of the Soviet censors, dissidents would steal x-ray prints from the dumpsters of hospitals to cut songs into with underground record presses. The sloppy discs would only play a few times before their shoddy craftsmanship led to their inevitable warping, but that wasn't what it was all about. It was the freedom the ribs provided that made them such a commodity and such a danger – the freedom to share ideas and emotions without state oversight. Artem didn't know that Sergei had been involved in that kind of musical black market, but it didn't surprise him.

As Artem slipped the bone music record onto his worn-down Victrola, a small part of him hoped that the vinyl had already deteriorated so far that he wouldn't have to confront his old mentor once more, but another shard of his heart yearned to hear Sergei's violin once more, after so many years apart.

Sergei had always told Artem, "When you need to make a choice and don't know which path to take, flip a coin – by the time it's halfway through the air, you'll know which side you hope it lands on." The coin was still spinning in the back of Artem's mind as he gently dropped the Victrola needle down onto the ribs' uneven grooves.

After a moment of crackling silence, the all-too-familiar hum of Sergei's Markneukirchen violin crept from the depths of the Victrola horn, washing over Artem with a sense of longing relief that only regret-stained nostalgia can create. Artem lowered himself back down into his armchair, closing his eyes as he allowed himself to be smothered by the melodic moans and tenor wails that called out from Sergei's record. This was not one of Kiselyov's bright springtime sonatas that the violinist had once played to commemorate the return of the sparrows to the trees of Kiev – this arrangement was haunting and mournful, full of heartache and woeful minor chords that wandered through the room like listless ghosts.

"My violin strings and my heart strings are one and the same," Sergei had once explained during one of his many philosophical musings as young Artem sat on the musician's canary couch, listening as intently as one would to a priest's sermon. "You cannot call music from one without the other." Just from listening to the instrument's sorrowful song, Artem knew that when Sergei had recorded this bone record, his heart must've been weeping.

Artem's eyelids slowly slid closed as he offered himself up to the sensation, allowing his spirit to be transported via violin bow back to the days of his youth. After that first day when Artem intruded on his musical maestro neighbor, the boy returned again and again to visit the magical Mr. Kiselyov. Sergei would provide him with gifts of warm tea and enchanting songs, while Artem brought him stories of his own devising in return – sometimes the boy's tales were plucked from his mother's storybooks or reinvented out of the old country legends or simply stories of strangers Artem passed on his way to the square. No matter the subject matter or the quality of Artem's clumsy retellings, Sergei was always happy to hear the boy's stories.

Eventually, Artem began to rely on Sergei for things outside of just his savant songweaving – Sergei showed him how to shave with a straight razor, how to set a table the proper way, how to stand with his back straight when talking to the pink-cheeked shop girl down the street. One year, he even agreed to serenade Artem's mother for her birthday when Artem didn't have any money to buy the hardworking woman even the smallest of gifts. Sergei Kiselyov quickly became a father to Artem, in all the ways that counted.

Even the arrival of the Germans hadn't been enough to silence Sergei the Songbird. In the quiet limbo of the witching hours, Artem would open his window and listen as Sergei stood on the roof of their apartment building and played a mournful melody for the city under siege. The violin's nimble notes echoed through the alleyways and bounced off the church spires with such grace that the Nazis could never pinpoint where the music was coming from – Kiev herself had become Sergei's patron, disguising his identity so that his serenades might continue to give the city hope in such bleak days. Artem even helped Sergei fashion a hidden compartment in the back of one of his stately bookshelves to hide his violin when the German commandos conducted one of their many inspections during the occupation.

When the city was finally liberated, Sergei played from dusk till dawn in Bessarabska Square, a caged bird free at last. Sergei had always been a revolutionary, fighting battles for the hearts and souls of men, and in those days Artem had been proud to help him. So, what changed?

"You know precisely what changed," a hoarse voice spoke from behind Artem's closed eyelids, shattering the bone music's tranquil trance! With a gasp, Artem's eyes shot open as his fingers dug into the cracked leather armrests — after all, he lived alone. He had locked the door. But nevertheless, a man was sitting in the chair across from him, staring intently as the ribs record wobbled on the spinning turntable.

Artem's vision struggled to adjust to the dark room — it had still been morning when he had returned from Nuck's market, but now the sky was black and starless, with only a few shards of errant moonlight to illuminate the shadowed sitting room. Where had the hours gone? He had only just started listening to the record…

"Fond memories will only get you so far," the silhouette spoke, its voice filled with a chilling calm that only served to make its words all the more menacing. "Until you have to look the truth in the eye."

Eye. Upon hearing that word, the frightened old Ukrainian finally dared meet the intruder's piercing gaze. Though his other features were still imperceptible amongst the sinister shadows, the man's eyes stuck out like starlight glinting from some far-away nebula… and when Artem looked harder, he realized that the irises were a frigid blue, like the color of the ice on the Dnieper River. They were eyes he couldn't forget, not even after thirty years — Sergei's eyes.

"*Vchytel*…," Artem muttered out a greeting as confusion stunned his senses. 'Vchytel' meant 'teacher', a title Artem had called Sergei many times back in the days of teatime and tribulations – it was the closest word to 'Papa' that the boy had been able to come up with. "What are you doing here?"

"That is no way to greet an old friend. I taught you better manners than that," Sergei spoke, an uncharacteristic undercurrent of malice running beneath his words. The man sitting in front of Artem – if he could be considered a man at all – was both corporeal and translucent, like a room full of cigarette smoke that had coalesced into a single image. Though he wore Kiselyov's robe and his very face, the Sergei sitting across from Artem was but the echo of the man who had once been, now no more than a reverberation sculpted from living shadow.

"I am here because you sought me out," Sergei's spirit elaborated with a cruel grin. "You bought the record, you dropped the needle. You wanted to find me."

"No, I – I mean," Artem stammered, searching for reason amongst the supernatural. Had he actually sought Sergei out? Was this all some self-imposed vision fueled by some secret desire for self-punishment? "I… I missed you. I missed our talks."

"As much as Judas missed sharing supper with Christ, I'm sure," Sergei clicked his tongue, dissatisfied with Artem's excuse. "But you were the reason our talks came to an end, weren't you, *Malish*? So, what is there to regret?"

"No, I – I mourned you," Artem replied, indignant as he refused such responsibility. "It was Captain Volkov that ordered that raid!"

"No, no of course. You only led the wolf to the den, you didn't feed," Sergei spat, his dark eyes narrowing as the shade stood up from his chair, casting an ungodly shadow across the hushed room. He seemed taller, his limbs more distended than they had been in life – and when he walked, dark streams of what appeared to be smoldering tar dripped from beneath his robe sleeves and from the soles of his naked feet, leaving behind a trail of burbling black bilge in his wake. "But what about Pietro? Is his blood not stained on your hands?"

"Pietro was…," As Artem began to construct another excuse, he released his clammy grip on his armchair for the first time – and when he looked into his hands, searching for an impossible answer, all he saw was black tar staining the skin of his own palms. Like the madness of Lady Macbeth, Artem scraped and tore at the black spot with his fingernails, but the ichor would not release its grip – it was bonded to the desperate man's flesh, marking him. "I didn't think… I was only doing my duty!"

"Oh, yes, your duty," Sergei growled as he stepped forward, now only a foot away from Artem. No matter how terrified Artem became or however badly he wanted to run for the door and take his chances out in the unnatural night, he found he couldn't budge from the chair, as if held by some invisible weight. "Your duty to the State? To the portraits of Stalin that peasants still hang in their kitchens decades after his death? Or do you mean your duty to the men with guns and badges that gave you a gun and a badge so you would feel important? Little people often confuse fear with power and will take whichever they can get – I just didn't expect you of all people to fall for such a trick."

"What about your duty to me, *Malish*," Sergei demanded as he violently gripped Artem's shoulder with a smoking black hand. Artem convulsed and groaned as he felt a cold pain spread from the points of Sergei's fingertips, veins of black blood cracking their way across the pale flesh of Artem's chest like imperfections twisting through a block of marble. "Where was the loyalty you owed the man who raised you? The man who protected you from the evils of the world lurking outside that apartment building? Where was your duty to him?!"

Sergei dug his fingers deeper into Artem's shoulder, causing the mortal man to finally cry out in agony as if the specre was jamming his thumb into a bullet wound. With tears streaming down his face and black veins creeping up his neck, Artem finally broke:

"Yes! I turned him in! It was me!" Artem howled his confession, his voice shuddering as a potent combination of fearful adrenaline and the release of repressed regret coursed through his body. "God, I'm sorry!"

"God can't forgive you," Sergei snarled with one final squeeze before finally releasing his lethal grip on Artem. "He wasn't the one you wronged."

As life gasped back into his body and the black veins receded, Artem's memories of that fateful day washed back over him like the waters of a long-overdue tide – a door left unlocked… a glimpse of two men locked in a passionate embrace… Sergei had always told him that Pietro was a colleague, a fellow musician and the only man who Kiselyov trusted to repair his cherished violin when it went out of tune. It was during the early days of Artem's service in the NVDK, when his superiors warned him again and again that homosexuals were dissidents and spies, set on corrupting the Soviet Ideal from the inside like a rot. This dogma had been beaten into him with such voracity that he actually believed it was true – he actually believed that he was saving Sergei from himself.

"I… I saw you and Pietro," Artem finally admitted, a puff of frosted breath escaping his lungs as the phantom musician circled behind him with his methodical steps. "I just walked in… I didn't think to knock… You had given me my own key to your flat years ago…"

"Why do you think that was? Perhaps it was because I trusted you," Sergei replied with the tone of a scolding teacher disappointed in their star student.

"I didn't know what to think," Artem admitted as the dagger of shame burrowed itself deeper in his chest. "I was in shock – I didn't know who to turn to –"

"So, you took any easy promotion by outing a celebrity and his partner to your death squad bosses," Sergei retorted, venom under his tongue.

"No! No, it wasn't like that!" Artem shouted, desperate for his old mentor to believe his words. "I never told them Pietro was with you! I knew bad things would happen if they knew you were… one of them. If I didn't report him, Pietro was going to get you caught! So, I told Captain Volkov where he could find Pietro and… and I made up a story about seeing him being intimate with another man in Navodnitsky Park."

"So, you knew a terrible fate would befall him, yet you threw Pietro to the dogs anyway."

"To protect you!" Artem cried, begging the shade to believe him. However, the only reply that came was Sergei's tar-slick fingers pressing against Artem's temples, sending a graveyard chill through the man's bones as the black veins began to spread towards his brain. The world swirled as Artem's vision began to tunnel, the haunting violin music still waltzing off the cursed record and dancing through the vacuous night, as if to taunt him.

"The State that you love so dear is built on a foundation of crumpled corpses and lies of omission," Sergei said as Artem's breaths became short and haggard under the spectre's touch. "You are just another bricklayer. So, I ask once more – why?"

"I– I–," Artem stuttered, his brain scrambled from the pain both present and remembered. Finally finding his way to a moment of lucidity, Artem wept like a boy as he confessed. "You kept him a secret from me! We had never kept secrets from each other, not since that first day I barged into your apartment and you offered me a seat. And in all the shock and the confusion, all I could think about was how you had kept Pietro a secret from me… I thought I was your son. I thought you could tell me anything! So, like the stupid, petulant child that I was, I only thought about how I could hurt you in return."

"I thought they would arrest Pietro, teach you both a lesson, and then they'd let him go and everything would go back to how things were. We could be happy again," Artem moaned, the agony in his heart dwarfing that of Sergei's touch. "But Captain Volkov didn't agree – whatever his reason, he had a personal vendetta against homosexuals. He sent Pietro out to Siberia, to the gulags… and I didn't speak up to stop him. When Pietro didn't come back, I knew that I had done something unforgivable."

"It was a flash of rage that only lasted for a second, but it has saddled me with shame and regret that I have carried with me for thirty years," Artem continued, finding a shred of freedom in this airing of traumatic truth. "My back aches and my knees buckle but I can never put it down. The weight of my betrayal. That was the moment when I learned there are things in life I can never take back. Please… please, forgive me."

The air was thick with a silent tension. Sergei released his grip on Artem's skull, slowly returning to stand in front of the broken man. When Artem summoned enough strength to look his mentor in the face, he found that the smoke encircling the shade's features had parted somewhat, revealing Sergei's face from beneath its shadowed veil for the first time since the bone music began. His blue eyes were red and tear stained at the edges, just like Artem's own.

"Pietro was taken to the gulag in Norlisk," Sergei explained, his voice having lost its grandeur, now stripped bare, his words as raw as an open wound in the night air. "They broke him with labor, beatings… but he kept fighting. Fighting to get back to me. But one night, he disobeyed some order or stepped over some line — he gave his jailers another empty excuse for punishment. A guard dragged him out into the snow in the middle of the night and left him there. Do you know how cold it gets in Norlisk?"

Artem shook his head, but he could guess. Norlisk was built in the Arctic Circle, the extreme temperatures serving as yet another weapon to be wielded against the USSR's prisoners.

"Thirty below zero," Sergei continued, answering his own question as the temperature in the sitting room seemed to drop another ten degrees. If Artem could've moved, he would've been shivering like a stray dog on a street corner — but he was still frozen, motionless in his chair. "Frostbite began to set in after only fifteen minutes, and hypothermia followed as his blood slowed and his brain froze. When they came to collect him in the morning, Pietro's stately nose, his delicate fingers that had restrung my bow with such grace, had turned black and crumbled away like the embers of a dead fire. He was still on his knees, petrified in the pose of a silent scream, begging to be heard. He had been dead for hours."

"I'm... so sorry," Artem forced out through the chokehold of tears that now gripped his throat like a noose. He had never learned of Pietro's true fate, but he had assumed the worst.

"Hear that?" Sergei asked, turning his head to the ribs record as the needle neared the homeland vinyl's center, signaling the impending end of the recording. As Artem listened, he realized that the violin music had stopped ages ago, and now instead he heard the sounds of water running and some sort of metallic clattering playing from the Victrola's horn. "When I received the news of my lover's death, I recorded this final sonata for Pietro... and for you. My heartbeat set its tempo, my blood inked each stanza – I pulled the music from the very marrow of my bones, as a good-bye to the two men I loved most in this world."

"That water in the background? It's my bathtub. It's where I opened my wrist with a straight razor just minutes after my final performance ended," As Sergei spoke, he lifted the sleeves of his robe to reveal a pair of deep gashes running from his wrist to the crook of his elbow on each arm, an endless drip of black tar cascading out from each gaping wound "This record contains my final breath, and thus, my very soul. Do you now understand why you chose to listen? What compelled you to take this record home?"

Artem nodded, devoid of any explanation or answer, adrift in a sea of grief.

"Do not cry, *Malish*," Kiselyov's phantom coaxed Artem with a disquieting comfort. "We are nearly done. Do you wish to hear the sonata I made for you? One last performance, for old times' sake."

Without waiting for an answer, the shade reached his black hand into his own breast, emerging from the impossible recesses within holding Sergei's old violin between his fingers. Conjuring a bow from the billows of smoke that surrounded him, the spectral musician began to play one final song for Artem. But it wasn't another funeral dirge – it was a soaring ballad, with the bombast of an entire orchestra contained in only four violin strings. As Artem listened, his heartbeat slowed and the screams of his mind faded away like sand smoothed by a wave's ebbing pull. As his eyes fluttered closed and sleep began to descend upon him, Artem realized that it was the song that Sergei had been playing the first day that they had met, when a bright-eyed seven-year-old eavesdropped on the maestro of Kiev. Then came a dreamless slumber.

When Artem opened his eyes, he felt a chilly breeze bite at his cheek and the tip of his nose... had he fallen asleep with a window left open? Had his haunting ordeal all been but a restless dream?

As Artem stirred, he found a weight pressing against his shoulder – but it was not the embrace of some warm blanket that had fallen upon him from the crown of his armchair. When he reached up to shed whatever lay atop him, Artem realized that it was metallic and freezing to the touch. His eyes shooting open, Artem was horrified to find himself not slumped in the sitting room of his apartment on the banks of the Dnieper River, but kneeling in a frozen tundra, surrounded by snow-buried barbed wire and crumbling brickwork ruins, a collar of impossibly heavy metal chains clamped tight around his neck!

Even as his skin began to painfully fuse to the icy iron restraints, there was nothing he could do to pry himself free. It was as if every moment he fought back, the chains became that much heavier upon his shoulders, smothering his will to fight as the Arctic chill sapped him of whatever strength remained in his old bones.

When he finally gave in and ceased his fruitless struggle, Artem realized that he was kneeling in the frozen ruins of what had once been the gulags of Norilsk… and all Artem could do was watch with frigid horror as a blizzard rolled in from the snow-capped mountains, ready to consume everything in its path in an embrace of cruel, endless white. Just before the howl of the storm winds deafened Artem, he swore he could hear the faint sounds of a violin, moaning on the breeze from somewhere far away…

TEN BLOCKS IN EASTWICK

IT WAS A WEDNESDAY IN ELIZABETH, NEW JERSEY – or Eastwick, as the natives are apt to call it. The East Coast had finally shrugged off the last shawl of winter and that afternoon was clear-skied and sunny. A sixty-degree March day was a godsend for the Eastwickers that had braved the gray December of 1965 and fought hard to see the other side. Classes had just let out a few minutes ago, the catholic academies and packed public schools emptying their adolescent prisoners out onto the leaf-lined sidewalks in their plaid skirts and abrasive wool sweaters, worn like winter fur reluctant to be shed.

Back then, Eastwick was one of the largest cities in the Garden State, its streets a mismatched patchwork of bricks and cathedrals, of Italians and Jews and Germans and Slavs – it was the crossroads where Jersey met the rest of the world, the little saucepan to New York City's melting pot. Despite its hustle and bustle, Elizabeth was a gentle giant – sure, there was crime, but nothing more than pickpockets and smalltime *famiglia* hustles running out of the back of butcher shops.

That afternoon, the Regent Theater was changing its marquee. As a sweat-spackled usher swapped out the letters for *The Rare Breed* and clumsily exchanged them for the syllables that made up the title of the new

Johnny Reno western, a man in a green coat passed beneath the theater's buzzing lightbulbs.

Many will go on to describe this Green Man in the days and years to come; they will talk about his ghoulish pale skin; about his eyes, beady and black and filled with some purpose only he knew; about the lifeless face that topped his massive, muscular frame that buckled at the corners of his neat appearance. Many would describe him, but three details would always be the same: he wore a green corduroy coat, a gray fedora, and on March 8th, he murdered a little girl.

Ten blocks away from the Green Man and his grim steps, seven-year-old Wendy Wolin kicked a pebble with her white shoetip as she swayed absentmindedly out front her apartment building steps. Her mother was inside – she had forgotten her wallet, and they needed it since they planned to get some shopping done before it was time to pick up Jodi, Wendy's older sister, from school. Wendy was a little Jewish girl, a shiny coat button of a child with big teacup-round eyes and chocolate-brown hair that was cut short and curled at the edges of her ears like a weaved flower crown. She wore a burgundy coat and little plaid dress that cascaded down from the frilled white collar folded neatly around her neck. Her collar was so tiny one could've mistaken it for a tea doily. She could've been dressed for temple or an afternoon at her grandmother's place, but Wendy did her best to hide from her mother how worn down her coat elbows had become – such was the price of a good playground escapade.

Eight blocks away from Wendy's idling, the Green Man committed his first violent act of the day. It would not be his last.

Seventh grader Diane DeNicola laughed with her friends as she strolled out of the gates of her Catholic school and made their way down to the little avenue of colorful storefronts, each window display vying to win the schoolchildren's hard-earned quarters after a long day of class. Sometimes they caught a movie at the Regent, but Diane couldn't read the half-built title on the marquee. She didn't have long to look.

Without warning, a brutal fist collided with Diane's orbital bone just beneath her eye, sending her small frame crumpling to the stone sidewalk with a sickening crunch! The teenage girl wailed on the ground and clutched her face as the crowd gasped, electrified into stillness by the sudden violent outburst. Diane's schoolgirl friends scattered, like a pack of mice watching one of their own snap their neck in a lethal trap. His knuckles bruised, the sallow Green Man kept walking, never speaking a word.

After a few stunned seconds, the onlookers wrestled themselves free from their shock and two men – a mechanic from the local garage and a bus rider that had been waiting on a nearby bench – sprinted after the Green Man to avenge Diane. The Green Man's black eyes narrowed, and his taut muscles propelled him into a dash, moving with a speed no one would've expected from a man of his stature. Ignoring his pursuer's shouts, the Green Man pivoted on his heels and ducked into a Woolworth's drugstore, hoping to lose his tails in the cacophony of retail aisles. The mechanic and the bus rider followed their mark, but the brute's sudden redirection had earned him a few seconds as the men stumbled to change course. When they burst into the Woolworth's, they were greeted by the jingle of the bell above the drugstore door… but no sign of the mystery attacker.

Not easily dissuaded, the bus rider pointed towards the rear of the shop, silently coaching the mechanic to loop around and cut the fugitive off before he could reach the back door. With a nod, the mechanic did as he was told, sneaking through the stationary aisle as the bus rider crouched and crept towards the far corner of the store, using the newspaper racks as cover as he grumbled about the Green Man's "head start".

The two pursuers inched towards the far corner of the pharmacy, boxing the Green Man in like hunting dogs converging on some grouse in tall grass. However, when they finally rounded the same aisle, fists ready for battle – the Green Man was gone, as if vanished into thin air! They searched the store and the nearby alleyways, but the Green Man had thoroughly given them the slip. Until their deaths decades later, the bus rider and the mechanic maintained that they would've seen Green Man if he had doubled back on them in the drugstore that day. And both men were adamant that the back door's bell never rang.

Seven blocks away from Wendy, the Green Man emerged like a phantasm from a shadowed recess in the brickwork and continued his march towards the heart of Eastwick.

At Wendy's apartment, her mother finally emerged onto the front stoop, grumbling as she fumbled through her jingling ring of keys to lock the deadbolt. She could never be too careful about that sort of thing. Wendy picked a dandelion out of a crooked crack at the spot where the sidewalk bricks met the asphalt of the street, but the fuzz blew away on the March wind before she could make a wish.

Four blocks away now, the Green Man stopped in front of a mother and daughter, Gina and Alisa Pasternak. Gina was finishing some grocery shopping before her husband returned from his New York commute and had decided to take Alisa with her, rather than leave her home alone for fear that the doe-eyed little girl would knock over another vase while playing. Now, the portly Polish mother felt a chill run through her marrow as she stood in the looming shadow of the gray-faced giant – a shadow under which she felt nothing good nor godly could ever grow. He mumbled something about "directions to the center of town", his voice sloshing, deep and dark in his throat, like someone trying to speak through a mouthful of spider eggs.

Gina opened her weather-chapped lips, trying to muster any sort of polite reply that would send the homunculus on his way and take his black eyes with him, but her tongue felt drier than it had a moment prior and the frightened sounds that escaped her throat were something short of human speech.

It wasn't until those midnight pinprick eyes shifted down and the Green Man gingerly rested his massive, ashen hand on little Alisa's soft shoulder that Gina felt a sense of fatal urgency return to her body. Maybe it was seeing that the Green Man's swollen, blood-flecked knuckles were each the size of just one of Alisa's vertebrae, or maybe it was watching as the Green Man opened his discolored lips and whispered, "Do you know the way?" to little Alisa, like the two were sharing a special secret to be kept from Mama.

Gina's steeled her composure, dug her recently-retouched nails into her daughter's arm and lead her away down the street, stabbing at the Green Man with words like daggers, but never daring to look the unnerving pedestrian directly in his warped face:

"Walk, don't talk."

With that, Gina and Alisa Pasternak quickly strolled away and across the street, leaving the Green Man silent and unrequited in their wake. But for whatever reason, he did nothing – no violence, no pursuit – perhaps a mother's protection warded him away like some boogeyman's curse, or perhaps his diseased consciousness had simply lost interest in this particular prey. He continued down the sidewalk.

Three blocks away, Wendy had finally run out of ways to entertain herself while waiting for her mother on the stoop. Mrs. Wolin had been distracted by a neighbor arriving home, and the two mothers had begun gabbing for what felt like interminable hours to the watch-hands of a seven-year-old. Seeing the boredom in her daughter's glassy eyes, Wendy's mother fished through her change purse and handed the girl a shiny silver quarter with an eagle on its back – a bribe to buy a Mr. Goodbar at the Woolsworth's when they finally made it downtown. But first, Wendy's mother needed to go around back and grab her car. Appeased by her mother's glinting tribute, Wendy agreed to just wait another minute out front for her mother to pull the car around.

A block away now, maybe less. The Green Man shoulder checked his way through a pack of strolling teenage girls, yelling at their eighteen-year-old Irish American leader, a tough bird named Clare Moran, "How in the bleedin' hell do you get to the center of town?!"

Clare and her friends scoffed, thinking the Green Man to be some yammering old wino let loose in the daylight hours – that is, until the Green Man reached Wendy Wolin's block.

Clare looked on as the massive man reached the peak of whatever personal lightning he was riding, right as he neared the Wolins' apartment steps. Wendy was standing now, using the stair bannister to balance like an off-kilter ballerina, but she quickly did away with such kiddy nonsense when she sensed someone was approaching. She turned towards the oncoming adult, her lily-smooth cheeks bunching up into a polite smile. Her mother had taught her it was the polite thing to do, even when you didn't know a person – she did it all the time at temple.

In reply to Wendy's beaming welcome, the Green Man unfurled his hand from the confines of his olive-shaded coat and laid a devastating blow straight to the petite girl's sternum! His hulking fist buried itself deep into her gut like a hit from a vengeful prizefighter – the Green Man's strike slammed the girl with such brute force that her feet lifted free from the sidewalk. Wendy collapsed to the ground as Clare and her clan shouted confused cries of protest. The Green Man made his swift exit as wordlessly as he had arrived.

His attack was unprovoked, unexplained, and unhinged – but getting clear answers suddenly becomes less important when there is a little girl lying prone in the street at your feet.

Clare and her girls ran to Wendy's side, scooping the shocked little girl up into their arms and running across the street to the Elizabeth Firehouse, since the police station was too far away. As the cavalcade of panicked youths burst into the fire chief's office, the starch-collared civil servant sputtered a heap of questions from beneath his silver mustache, namely:

"What the hell happened to the girl?"

All Wendy said was: "A man punched me."

She was confused but didn't show a tinge of pain. Her porcelain face didn't crack, the light didn't leave her big green eyes. It wasn't until the chief noticed crimson stains dribbling onto the crisp stationary scattered across his desk that they unbuttoned Wendy's hand-me-down coat and found her plaid dress wet – saturated with dark blood. There had been no punch – Wendy Wolin had been stabbed. The blade was so sharp and the wound so deep that she didn't even feel it pierce her chest.

In that moment, Wendy had no way of knowing that she was already dead.

Four blocks away, the Green Man kept running, humid, pungent breaths escaping his gnarled gray lips as he ran in search of nothing, in fear of everything. The fire chief sent a motorcycle cop out to run down young Ms. Wolin's attacker as they raced Wendy to Elizabeth General Hospital. The once-tranquil Eastwick storefronts were assaulted by the angry red glare of the emergency vehicle lights as they screamed towards their destination, just out of reach. The EMTs did their best to disguise their fear as they realized that the blade that impaled Wendy had not only drawn blood, but had punctured her liver and her right lung in its single, ruthless plunge.

Ten blocks away. The Green Man banged on the door of an inactive bus, searching for an escape. The bus driver reported that the madman stared at him – no, rather, through him – with those black button eyes, gibbering a slurry of words only his sick brain could understand. "Looked like he was on Cloud Nine," the disturbed driver would later say.

The number of blocks don't matter now. After his ravings by the bus, the Green Man vanished into the cobweb of Eastwick side streets and back alleys. His hunting knife would be found the next day in a storm drain gutter half a block away from the Wolin's stoop, its blade still crusted with child-blood. Over the next weeks and months, 1,500 suspects would be questioned in the largest manhunt in the history of New Jersey. Every police station in the country was provided with their own share of wanted posters, adorned with the ashen, lifeless face of the Green Man, his haunting eyes staring out from the black ink.

But the Green Man would never be seen again.

An hour after she was picking dandelions from out of cracks in her front stoop, Wendy Sue Wolin was pronounced dead. She still had her mother's quarter in her pocket, untouched, untarnished, and unspent.

Ever since, the shade of Wendy Wolin has hung over the streets of Eastwick, the senseless violence of it all cauterizing the wound of her murder into the very flesh of Elizabethtown. Her case remains open to this day – a poltergeist never to be exorcised from the shadowed history of the great Garden State.

As time has passed, the man in the green coat has become a boogieman to those who were children in Eastwick during 1966, and his phantom has passed hereditarily to their children, and their children after them, like a rot unable to be fully burnt away. Conspiracies have swirled around that March afternoon like flies to a carcass: some think the Green Man was a mob hitman from Highland Park, sent to kill Wendy as recompense for the transgressions of another member of the Wolin family, while other theorists guess that he could've been an escaped mental patient in the throes of a mind-altering psychosis. Others still believe that he was the son of a prominent funeral home director with a propensity for breaking women, but he was protected by his father's weighty contributions to Mayor Dunn's election campaign.

In the 1990s, a man was questioned by the Elizabeth Police after finding that he matched the Green Man's description, suffered from violent mental illness, and was in the area of the Wolins' apartment the day of the killing. But after he passed two polygraphs with little more than a smirk, the investigators had no option but to release him, despite the fact that the Assistant Prosecutor on Wendy's case believed, "without a shadow of a doubt", that he was the murderer.

Was this man an unhinged malcontent, or does the sheer brutality of his actions that day lead him into the realm of something darker – a vessel of hatred, possessed by a black hand of unknowable evil? Was this killing to satiate some horrid urge deep from within his gullet, or to appease some dark god with whom only he communed?

Fifty years after that March afternoon, it seems we are destined to never know the Green Man's true purpose or the reason that robbed Eastwick of Wendy Wolin's light. She was a little candle, her flame flittering in the spring air, her wick barely curled, her wax not yet spent – but nonetheless, Wendy was extinguished by a cold wind on March 8th, 1966. And no matter what answer is gleaned or what truth you subscribe to, her light will never be reignited.

Note from the Author

*Most of the stories in **High Strangeness** are tales of fiction, meant for scares and creeps and the like – but I assure you, the sad story of Wendy Wolin is unfortunately very true (save for a few small narrative embellishments for the sake of storytelling). I grew up in Scotch Plains, NJ, only a few miles from Elizabeth, and this case has remained a scar on Eastwick, Wendy's family, and New Jersey itself for more than fifty years. The case remains open and Wendy's sister, Jodi, the last surviving member of the Wolin family, is still actively searching for answers to the senseless loss of her sister. I only hope that our telling of this sorrowful tale will bring more attention to this tragedy, and hopefully, some closure.*

If you have any relevant information regarding the case, I urge you to contact the <u>New Jersey Office of the Attorney General tip line:</u> (1-800-277-2427).

We can't bring Wendy back, but we can give her story an ending.x

DEATH AT YOUR DOOR

Ever since you were born
There's been a man at your door
No matter where the road of life meets you
Death is on your front stoop, ready to greet you.

Death is in your kitchen, by that loose socket plug
Or at the bottom of that bottle you're ready to chug
Death's behind the wheel of your old pickup truck
But he'll be a quiet passenger, if you've got enough luck.

Death is floating gently out back in your pool
I hope you're a good swimmer, I hope you're no fool
Death lurks in the thunderclouds, ready to strike
You better have an umbrella on this most auspicious night.

Death is hiding in the hearts of men
They've killed before, he knows they'll do it again
But Death isn't evil, like real people are
If you're out looking for him, you won't have to look far.

Because Death is in the flower buds, ready to bloom
Death is a cycle, not simply some doom
Death stands at your bedside, this much is true
But without old man Death, we'd have nothing new.

They'd be no new birds flying from their nests in the Spring
There'd be no new scents, no new songs to left sing
Without Death, we'd all just grow old
And how boring that life would be, at least so I'm told.

Death is waiting for you, here at the end
In times like these, he knows everybody needs a friend
And though you can't see a smile across his white skull
He knows you lived life to the fullest, that your time wasn't dull

He hopes it's been full of love and joy
For he's been watching over you all, each girl and boy
He's been watching and waiting, and keeping you safe
Till your time finally came to see the old reaper's face

And now at the finish, he hopes that you're glad
That you lived with such courage, took the good with the bad
Though he can't tell you where your spirit is bound
He'll knows he'll see you again on the next time around.

SPECIAL THANKS

David & Melissa Tice

Elsa Ames

Steven Collins

Btooke Solomon

Max Zell

Ciarán O' Donovan

David Magee & the Brass Mantle Family

The Buck Family

ABOUT THE AUTHOR

PHIL TICE IS AN AMERICAN AUTHOR, artist, and filmmaker, originally hailing from the Great State of New Jersey where he grew up surrounded by local legends like the Jersey Devil and the Feltville Witches. One Halloween, Phil was dared to watch *The Exorcist* with some middle school friends and the rest was history. Phil began his love affair with horror as a child with books like *Goosebumps* and *Scary Stories to Tell in the Dark,* and movies like *The Thing* and *Return of the Living Dead.* Phil began writing and self-producing films with his friends in high school, creating their own homemade version of Cannon Films in the suburbs of Central Jersey and paving the road for Phil's career in entertainment.

Phil went on to hone his craft at Boston's Emerson College, where he graduated with a BFA, and now lives in Hollywood, California, where he makes his living as a director and screenwriter. When entering the film industry, he learned how to bring monsters to life on set as a special effects makeup artist before becoming a fully-fledged horror filmmaker in his own right. He has collaborated with horror icons like Thom Mathews (*Return of the Living Dead, Friday the 13th*) and Cary Woods (*Scream, Godzilla*) and currently works for Oscar-nominated screenwriter and mentor David Magee (*Life of Pi, Finding Neverland*).

Phil considers authors like Stephen King, Neil Gaiman, and William Peter Blatty to be some of his greatest inspirations, and he hopes that a few of their fingerprints show through in his own humble stories.

Pictured: Phil with his father and frequent horror movie sacrifice, David, on the set of Phil's movie, *Stain-Free: Code Black*.

Enjoyed *High Strangeness?*

Check out

TICE TOMES

to find more stories by Phil Tice,
as well as prints and apparel featuring original horror art!